Katy's Wild Foal

Katy's Wild Foal

Victoria Eveleigh

Illustrated by Chris Eveleigh

Orion
Children's Books

ORION CHILDREN'S BOOKS

First published in Great Britain under the title *Katy's Exmoor* in 2002 by Tortoise Publishing
This edition first published in 2012 by Orion Children's Books
This edition published in 2017 by Hodder and Stoughton

11

Text copyright © Victoria Eveleigh, 2002, 2012
Illustrations copyright © Chris Eveleigh, 2002, 2012

The moral rights of the author and illustrator have been asserted.

A CIP catalogue record for this book
is available from the British Library.

ISBN 978 1 44400 541 7

Printed and bound in Great Britain
by Clays Ltd, Elcograf S.p.A.

The paper and board used in this book are
made from wood from responsible sources.

Orion Children's Books
An imprint of
Hachette Children's Group
Part of Hodder and Stoughton
Carmelite House
50 Victoria Embankment
London EC4Y 0DZ

An Hachette UK Company
www.hachette.co.uk

www.hachettechildrens.co.uk

For Sarah and George, with love

Exmoor

BRISTOL CHANNEL

COMBE MARTIN
PARRACOMBE
LYNTON
BRENDON
MALMSMEAD
PORLOCK
MINEHEAD
BLACKMOOR GATE
CHALLACOMBE
DUNSTER
SIMONSBATH
WHEDDON CROSS
EXFORD
WINSFORD
WITHYPOOL
HAWKRIDGE
TWITCHEN
DULVERTON

Contents

1

Born on the Moor

Katy sat alone at the kitchen table, staring blankly at the birthday presents in front of her. A cheerful weather man on the TV was forecasting snow on high ground. Katy knew it was the last thing they needed at lambing time, but a part of her longed for the excitement of snow.

My birthday will always be in the middle of lambing, she thought gloomily. Why couldn't I have been born in the summer? Even Christmas Day would have been better than the first day of April.

Lambing was a hectic time of year at Barton Farm,

so Katy's family were too busy to organise a party or an outing somewhere for her. Today they'd done their best, she had to admit. They'd even said she could invite someone over for the day, but she hadn't been sure who to ask. She didn't really have a best friend.

Gran and Granfer had come round for the afternoon, so that had been fun. She'd helped Gran make a trifle. Everyone had stopped for tea, complete with trifle and cake. For a moment it had felt like a proper birthday.

Now it was early evening. Gran and Granfer had gone back home, and Mum, Dad and Katy's older brother, Tom, had gone outside to catch up on all the work that needed to be done before darkness fell. The house felt cold and empty.

Katy took the iPod her parents had given her out of its box. She'd have to ask Tom to set it up for her when he came in again, as the instructions were impossible to understand. What she'd really wanted was a mobile phone – everyone at school had one, except her. But her parents said mobiles were a waste of money because there was no signal at Barton Farm. Katy put the iPod back in its box, looked briefly at a jewellery-making kit Auntie Rachel had given her and then picked up an old book called *Moorland Mousie*. She turned the thick, yellowing pages. There were some lovely illustrations, but the writing looked rather heavy going. She found reading hard work.

"Take care of this book. I hope you'll love it as much as I did at your age," Granfer had said when he'd given it to her.

"What's it about, Granfer?" she'd asked, thumbing through the pages.

"It's the life story of an Exmoor pony called Mousie. A bit like the story of Black Beauty, but much better in my opinion," Granfer had replied. "That book started my lifelong interest in Exmoor ponies."

"Have Exmoors been at Barton forever?"

"Well, I don't know about forever," he'd said, smiling. "But they've been here for as long as I can remember, and way before that I expect. Your great grandfather was a founding member of the Exmoor Pony Society, you know. Loved his Exmoors, he did, and he was determined they should stay as they've always been. He was even against me having one to ride when I was a boy. 'Their place is on the moor, living as nature intended,' he used to say. Free-living, it's called nowadays. It means they live like wild ponies but they're actually owned and managed by someone, so they're not truly wild – not like deer, foxes and other wildlife."

The Barton herd of registered Exmoor ponies was one of the oldest and best herds in the country, and Granfer was a highly respected member of the Exmoor Pony Society. It was a great sadness to him that his son, Katy's father, had no interest in the herd. The farm had been handed over to Dad, but Granfer still owned the ponies.

Gran and Granfer had lived at the farm until last year, but Gran couldn't cope with the stairs anymore so they'd moved to a bungalow. Now they only visited a couple of times a week, and Katy missed them terribly. Barton Farm was an isolated place, surrounded by the high moors, several miles from the nearest town. She often felt lonely and cut off from other people her own age. Most of the children at school lived in town, and the girls were mainly into fashion and music, which really didn't interest her much, although she'd learned to pretend it did. Tom was nine years older than she was, and all he talked about was farming. He seemed to know exactly what he was going to do with his life: he'd go to agricultural college and then help Dad farm Barton. One day the farm would be his.

Katy put the book down and picked up the jewellery kit. The box slipped out of her hand as she tried to open it, and hundreds of beads and fake jewels spilled out.

"Oh, no!" she squeaked, watching in disbelief as they hit the floor and sprayed out in all directions like a multi-coloured firework.

What do I do now? I'll lose them completely if I use the vacuum cleaner. I'd better find a dustpan and brush, she thought.

The beads were surprisingly slippery. Katy nearly fell several times as she tried her best to gather them together. They seemed to have other ideas, shooting off in all directions as soon as the brush touched them. Eventually she managed to round most of them up and crammed a rather unpleasant mixture of beads, jewels, dust and dog hairs back into the box.

I can't face sorting it all out now, she thought. I may as well walk up to the lambing shed and see if I can help. The orphan lambs will need feeding soon. I'll go and give them a birthday cuddle. Perhaps they'd like a little bit of cake.

Katy took a piece of birthday cake, wrapped it in some foil and put it in the pocket of Tom's old army jacket which was hanging on the back of the chair. The jacket smelt overpoweringly of sheep and was far too big for her, but she put it on anyway. It saved having to hunt around for her own coat, and wearing Tom's clothes made her feel like a proper farmer. She went to the hallway, took off her cosy sheepskin boots – a birthday present from Gran – and winced as she slipped her bare feet into her chilly, damp wellies.

Socks really would have been a good idea, she said to herself. Oh well, too late now. I won't be outside for long, anyway.

She opened the door and stepped out into the sleety rain. Behind her, the door slammed before she had a chance to turn and shut it herself.

Cold drops hit Katy's warm face. Going from warm and dry to cold and wet was always horrible. Screwing her face up against the weather, she trudged along the muddy track to the lambing shed, which was a beacon of light in the darkness.

Nobody was in the shed, but Katy noticed a ewe in the corner straining and grunting loudly. She didn't know what to do, so she decided to stay and keep an eye on things for a few minutes, hoping someone would come.

No one came, and no lamb came out of the ewe. As she stood there, Katy noticed a newborn lamb nearby who didn't seem to know who its mother was. One ewe kept butting it whenever it went near her, and two others weren't sure if it was theirs or not. The poor lamb looked so wet and bewildered. Perhaps its mother was the one trying to give birth in the corner. Above the roar of the wind, Katy thought she could hear the tractor in the direction of the Common, so she left the sanctuary of the shed and went to find help.

The wind in the fields was even stronger than it had been on the way up to the shed. It snatched Katy's breath away and made Tom's wet jacket slap against her body. Underfoot, the ground was uneven and slippery. To add to her discomfort, the rain started to trickle down into her wellies, surrounding her bare feet with ice-cold water. With every step she took, the combination of bare feet, water and rubber boot made a rude squelching noise which at any other time would have had Katy in fits of laughter.

She reached the Common gate, but there was still no sign of the tractor, although she thought she could hear the rumble of its engine. Perhaps it was only the wind she could hear.

The Common was a large area of moorland on which Barton Farm and other neighbouring farms had grazing rights for sheep, cattle and ponies. It was here that the Barton herd of Exmoor ponies lived all year round.

Katy leaned against the gate and peered through its bars.

Water ran in a shallow sheet off the saturated surface of the moor, forming tiny rivers in the sheep tracks and making ponds against the boundary walls. A wide stream flowed through the gateway where Katy stood. Beyond the gate, she could see the outline of her den – a dark grey shape against the lighter grey of the rain-soaked moor and cloud-laden sky.

The den was a group of gorse bushes that had grown together and had been eaten by sheep so that they formed a circular shelter with a hollowed-out middle. Katy had made it her own special place, and she'd spent many happy hours playing there.

She was just about to turn for home when she spotted something moving on one side of the den. It looked like the back half of an Exmoor pony, with its head and neck hidden from view in the circle of gorse. Katy remembered Granfer saying ponies sometimes left the herd if they were sick or foaling. She opened and closed the gate with difficulty, and walked up to the den. It was odd that, as she approached, the pony didn't move. Perhaps it was caught up or injured. When Katy was only a few steps away, the mare leaped backwards and started whinnying in a low, agitated voice.

"Oh!" gasped Katy.

A tiny foal's head poked out of the bushes, followed by four matchstick legs which shakily supported a skinny body. Its bony frame seemed to be shrink-wrapped in dark, wet skin, and it looked impossibly thin and fragile. The foal started to walk with wobbly steps towards Katy, and she was spellbound as it came right up to her. She reached out and just managed to touch its tiny forehead with her frozen fingertips before the mare whinnied anxiously and the foal realised its mistake and hurried away. In an instant, the magical moment was lost and the mare and foal had disappeared over the brow of the hill.

Katy realised she was shaking all over with cold and her hands, feet and face hurt. If she felt like this, what must the little foal feel like? It wouldn't be able to survive outside, not in this weather. She'd have to get Dad to bring it back to the farm, and she'd look after it.

Filled with new purpose, Katy ran most of the way back home. She'd forgotten all about the lambs, and the ewe trying to give birth in the shed.

Katy walked into the kitchen to find Dad flat on his back having slipped on some of the beads she hadn't managed to pick up.

Her mum was plugging in the vacuum cleaner. "Where have you been, Katy? We've been looking for you everywhere! I even rang Gran and Granfer to see if you went back with them, so now I've worried them unnecessarily too. Oh my goodness, you're soaked to the skin! What have you been up to?" she asked.

"And the next time you want to try killing me, choose a method that's a little less painful, please," said Dad, climbing unsteadily to his feet.

"I'm sorry, I was looking for you, so I went up to the Common and I found . . ."

"Why on earth did you think we'd be on the Common at this time of night? We were feeding the cows in Broadacre," Dad interrupted.

"What were you thinking of, leaving these beads all over the place?" Mum added. "We've got enough to do without this sort of mess, and Dad nearly had a nasty accident."

"Nearly!" Dad exclaimed. "It feels as if I've done

myself a permanent injury."

At that moment, Tom came in from looking round the sheep in the fields. "One dead lamb – a fox has taken most of it – and a lame one, which I injected and marked, and I brought those twins we were worried about back to the shed because they're not getting enough milk." He turned to Katy. "So that's where my jacket got to! How many times have I got to tell you not to take my things without asking?"

The conversation was not going as Katy had planned, and she tried to alter its direction before everyone started telling her off at once. "I'm really sorry, honestly I am," she said. "You see, I went up to the Common and found this tiny foal which must have been born today. It's going to die if we don't bring it in!"

"I'm sorry, Katy, but there's no way I'm going out on the Common to get a mare and foal in tonight," said Dad. "The foal wouldn't be able to walk all the way back to the farm, for a start. And the mare has never been parted from the herd or stabled, so she'd probably get so distressed that she'd end up accidentally trampling her baby or something. They're much better off where they are. Besides, every inch of shed space is taken up with ewes and lambs at present."

"But Dad!" sobbed Katy, "It'll die out there, I know it will!"

"Well, that's just a chance we'll have to take, love,"

Dad said wearily.

Katy's mum sighed. An argument like this was the last thing they needed. "Exmoor ponies are very good at surviving in awful weather, you know. Their ancestors lived during the Ice Age," she said.

"I don't want a history lesson! I want to save my foal!" cried Katy.

"Crikey, it's *your* foal now, is it?" Tom teased.

"Shut up Tom, you're not helping," hissed Dad.

"Yes! Shut up, Tom!" shouted Katy, and she burst into tears. Her hands and feet had become unbearably painful as they'd started to thaw out, and she was terribly disappointed. Why couldn't they see how serious this was? She ran up to her bedroom and banged the door.

"Happy Birthday," whispered Mum.

"Oh dear," sighed Dad. "I'd better take a look, I suppose."

Dad put on his coat and boots, collected some hay and went off on the quad bike to look for the mare and foal. After an hour of searching, he found them sheltering by a hedge. The foal was suckling the mare, but he had to admit that it looked very frail.

Its mother looked thin, too. Bad weather and not enough milk were often a lethal combination for early foals. Taking care not to frighten the mare, he placed the hay nearby. It was the best he could do at that time of night. Besides, he'd been away from the lambing shed for too long. He'd check on them both again in the morning.

"Sorry, little fella," he said to the foal. "You'll just have to take your chance."

The shed was in chaos. Five ewes had given birth. One had produced a good, strong single lamb. Three had produced twins which all looked identical, or perhaps they were actually a single, twins and a set of triplets, or even two singles and a set of quadruplets. Another had two lambs already, and was trying to give birth to a third one which was coming backwards. The abandoned lamb Katy had seen a couple of hours ago was wandering about, cold, hungry and bewildered. Several sheep who were about to give birth were adding to the confusion by trying to claim babies which weren't theirs. There were only two spare individual pens left for newborn lambs and their mothers. In a big pen in the corner, lit by the red glow of a heat lamp, the hungry orphans bleated noisily.

Dad sighed heavily. His back ached from the fall on Katy's beads, and he felt shattered. "Damn the Exmoor ponies," he muttered as he set about sorting things out. A long night lay ahead.

2

A White Easter

"Why did I wish for snow?" thought Katy, looking out of her bedroom window at the transformed view. She'd been ill with an ear infection for three days now, ever since her birthday, and each fresh fall of snow had made her even more worried about the foal. Dad had been to see it each day, making a detour when he went round the ewes and lambs. He'd reported to Katy that the foal was alive and well, but she could tell he was concerned about it.

While she was ill, Gran and Granfer had come to the farm to keep Katy company. Granfer had read her the whole of *Moorland Mousie*, and she couldn't get the story out of her head. In her feverish state she'd experienced weird dreams, most of them centred around ponies. In one of her dreams she was a pony herself and could talk to the others in the herd.

The following day, she'd asked Granfer if ponies could speak to each other.

"That's a difficult one," he'd replied. "They do, but not in the same sort of way as us. They only use their voices when they're very excited or too far away to use body language. It makes sense, if you think about it. A prey animal like a pony, which predators may want to eat, will use its voice as little as possible, so it doesn't advertise its whereabouts."

"What's body language?"

"We use body language all the time," Granfer had explained. "When we smile or scowl, or jump for joy, or shuffle along sulking, for instance. Horses have developed it down to a fine art, though, because it's the main way they communicate with each other. Next time you see the herd, stand still and watch the ponies. You'll see that they very rarely actually bite or kick each other, but they communicate all the time with their bodies. If you can learn to copy them you'll be half way to speaking their language."

"That's silly! How can I put my ears back or swish my tail like a horse?"

Granfer had laughed. "Yes, I agree, there are limits to what you can do. To a horse, a human looks like a predator, so horses are naturally frightened of people. But it's amazing how you can overcome that fear by using your body in the right way."

"How d'you mean?"

"Well, if you face a pony, look it in the eye, and make sudden movements, that's threatening. If you want to be friendly, don't look directly at it and move around in a relaxed way. With a nervous pony, a good trick is to walk towards it, retreat a few paces and then go back again, getting a little closer every time. No predator walks away from its prey, you see."

Katy had listened, concentrating as hard as she could.

"The trouble is that human body language is often totally different, so we give out the wrong messages. For instance, a girl who runs up to her pony with her arms outstretched is saying, 'I want to hug you' in human language, but the poor pony is more likely to think she's saying, 'I want to catch you and kill you', so it runs away or, worse, kicks out at the girl. Then everyone thinks the pony is badly behaved. A lot of problems with horses are due to misunderstandings like that. The key to understanding horses is to try seeing the world from their point of view."

There and then, Katy had decided to learn horse language.

*

15

On the day before Easter, Katy felt well enough to get up. She was determined to go out and see the foal for herself, whatever her parents said, so she put on lots of warm clothes and a thick pair of socks.

As she went downstairs for breakfast she could hear her parents talking. She sat on the stairs and listened.

"At least you can get permission to feed the ponies some hay now there's snow on the ground, Phil," said Mum.

"I wish it were that simple," replied Dad. "It's Saturday today and a bank holiday on Monday, so I doubt if there'll be anyone in the office to give permission until Tuesday."

"Well, I think they'll understand if we just go ahead and do it, especially with a mare and foal in danger of dying if nothing's done. Oh! Hello Katy, love. Feeling better?" said Mum, stopping the conversation abruptly.

"Much better. What's all this about the foal?" asked Katy.

"I'm afraid the mare's milk could be drying up. This weather seems to be testing both of them a bit," Dad said gently.

"Can I go and see them?" Katy half-whispered.

"You might find it rather upsetting, love," Dad warned.

"I promise I'll try to be brave," Katy replied, "but I've got to see them."

Half an hour later, Katy was sitting behind Tom on the quad bike, holding his army jacket tightly as they sped over the Common. With her face against Tom's broad back, she occasionally caught the unmistakable whiff of sheep from his jacket. A small trailer laden with hay bumped along behind them. Moss, the sheepdog, ran ahead, apparently oblivious to the freezing snow underfoot.

It had stopped snowing and the wind had eased, but it was still bitterly cold. The colourless landscape looked like an old black and white photograph; the white snow casting the dark gorse bushes and trees into black silhouettes, capped by the dark grey sky.

Katy could tell that Tom was just going through the motions of looking for the foal. He probably thought it was dead. She dreaded finding it, but knew they had to.

"Look!" Tom shouted, stopping the bike and pointing at the ground.

Katy looked. A line of small craters in the snow – some larger ones with several tiny ones mixed in – ran in the direction of a steep valley to the right.

"Unless another foal's been born, that's them," Tom said, starting the engine again.

She wrapped her arms around his waist as he opened up the throttle and followed the tracks. There was no time to worry about what they might find – Katy was too busy clinging on as Tom navigated through drifts and swerved round hummocks.

They found the mare and foal down in the valley, and dropped a bale of hay on the ground nearby. The foal was still like a walking skeleton, but at least it was alive.

Looking at Katy and Tom warily out of the corner of her eye, the mare came to the hay and started to eat, gathering great bunches into her mouth and munching steadily. The foal nudged around its mother's flanks and then suckled.

"She's still got some milk, by the looks of it," said Tom, shoving his hands into his jacket pockets.

The foal stopped suckling, splayed out its hind legs and relieved itself.

"Looks like she's a filly foal," said Tom.

Since her birthday, Katy had daydreamed constantly about the adventures she'd have with her pony. They'd be inseparable, and they'd win all the prizes at shows. Now there was the thrilling possibility of breeding other foals, if everything went according to plan. "Ideal! I hoped it was! I mean I hoped *she* was!" Katy's words tumbled together in her excitement. "Oh, she's just perfect! Dad's got to let me keep her. He will let me keep her, won't he, Tom?"

"I should wait and see if she lives first," said Tom. He glanced at his sister, and added, "Well, she's survived this long, so there's a good chance, but you know what Dad thinks about having ponies back at the farm. He says they're worse than locusts, and they spoil any field you put them in." He pulled a squashed, foil-wrapped parcel out of his pocket. "Is this something to do with you?"

"My birthday cake!" Katy exclaimed. "I'd forgotten all about it! I was going to give some to the orphan lambs."

"Lambs don't eat cake, you daft dipstick," Tom said, shaking it out onto the ground before scrunching the foil into a ball and stuffing it into his pocket as he walked back to the trailer.

"Well, foals do!" whispered Katy.

With tentative steps, the foal walked up to the cake and nibbled a few crumbs from the surface of the snow. She looked at Katy, nodded a few times as if saying, "Yes, that's good!" and then searched about for more. When she raised her head again, snow crystals were stuck to the whiskers around her tiny mouth.

Katy giggled, and the foal gave a quick, high-pitched whinny in reply.

Tom glanced up the valley. "Look out! Here come the others! Quick, help me put the rest of the hay up there, then hopefully they won't disturb these two."

The ponies came trotting down the valley, eyes bright, ears pricked, necks arched and manes bouncing like flickering flames. Katy wondered why she had never found them special before. At that moment, they were the most beautiful creatures she'd ever seen. A few yards away they checked, blowing down their noses suspiciously at Katy, Tom and Moss. Then the boldest mare came forward and started eating, quickly followed by all the others, jostling and squealing. The stallion made sure he had a large lump of hay to himself. As the competition increased, some of the ponies decided to shift closer to the mare and foal.

"Oh no!" exclaimed Katy. "They'll knock her over!"

She needn't have worried. The foal's mother kept the other mares away from her baby, and they seemed to respect her even though she was obviously weaker than they were. Katy studied their body language, fascinated.

"Come on," said Tom. "Time to go home. I've got strict instructions not to let you get cold."

As Katy climbed aboard the quad bike, she glanced back at the ponies feasting on the hay and wished she could take a photo of the scene. Instead, she stored it away in her head – a memory to stay with her for life.

*

More snow fell on the night before Easter. Dad, Mum and Tom were exhausted from trying to keep as many young lambs as possible warm and dry, and they were beginning to lose a lot of older ones out in the fields. Now that there was snow on the ground, Dad could see exactly what wild animals had been prowling around the fields. He was alarmed by the amount of fox and badger prints. Many of the dead lambs were half-eaten but, as usual, it was a job to know whether they'd been killed or they'd died of cold.

Whichever way, it was a depressing business, and it meant there'd be far fewer lambs to sell in the autumn than he'd promised the bank manager. Money was a constant worry, and just lately Dad had started to think the unthinkable: they might have to sell the farm if things didn't improve.

Tom and Katy fed the ponies again on Easter morning. They were waiting expectantly in the valley. Katy studied them all intently, and was sure the mare and foal were a little bit stronger.

Gran and Granfer came over for the day, and Katy's Auntie Rachel came to lunch with her boyfriend, Mark. Rachel had lived at Barton Farm until a couple of years ago, when she'd moved to work in a hunter livery yard. Mark's family rented a farm nearby, and Mark lived and worked there.

Unlike her older brother, Rachel had always loved horses and was a very good rider. When she was a teenager she'd been in lots of Pony Club teams. Now she had a reputation for being able to train horses that most people considered impossible to handle.

Katy waited until her father had finished eating his roast dinner. It's now or never she thought. "Can I have that foal on the moor, Dad?" It felt like a pre-recorded message playing in her head. She couldn't really believe she was actually saying it!

"Well, I don't see why not," said Dad. "If she passes her inspection at branding time, she can join the herd and we'll call her yours. How about that?"

"No, I mean can I keep her at the farm and break her in and ride her? Can I have her as my own pony?"

"What a good idea!" Granfer said. "As I still own the ponies, I'd like to give you the foal. Call it a late birthday present."

Dad glowered at Granfer. "That's all very well, but it will be eating my grass and using up my shed space," he said.

"*She*," said Katy.

"What?" Dad frowned at her. He looked confused and tired, and Katy suddenly wished she'd said nothing. Too late now.

"*She* will be eating your grass, not it."

"She, then," said Dad. "No, I'm sorry, Katy, but you can't have her here on the farm for all sorts of reasons. Apart from anything else, I don't want you getting hurt. Exmoors aren't beginners' ponies, especially if they've been born wild. Granfer knows as well as anybody that it takes a lot of work to get them to accept humans at all, and they'll always keep that wild streak in them. I learned to ride on an Exmoor, and it bucked me off so many times that I was put off riding . . ."

"What nonsense," Granfer interrupted. "When I was a lad, all the farm children learned on Exmoors, and damned good riders it made them too. Rachel did all her Pony Club competitions on an Exmoor when she was a little girl. You just never took to ponies – always preferred machines for some reason. It would be good fun to do a bit of pony breaking again, and Rachel could help as well."

"Just like old times, eh?" Rachel said, smiling at Granfer.

Dad looked crestfallen, like he always did when reminded by Granfer of how good at riding Rachel was and how disappointingly bad he was. "There's also the problem of where it, *she*, is going to live," he said. "She'll be miserable without company, and she'll need a stable, with straw and hay. And it doesn't stop there: saddle, bridle, vet's bills . . ."

"I'll save all my money," Katy said quickly. "I got ten pounds for my birthday from Auntie Anne."

Dad looked at her as if to say ten pounds wouldn't go very far, but he said, "Okay, then. You can have that foal after she's weaned this autumn if, *and only if*, she passes her inspection. That means she'll be fully registered, so if she's impossible to train, or you lose interest in her, she can go back and run with the herd on the Common. If she doesn't pass the inspection, she gets sold. Deal?"

Katy jumped up from her chair and gave her dad a hug. "Deal!" she replied.

3

Alice

As Katy got onto the school bus on the first day of the summer term, it seemed that lambing, the snow and her foal had been a dream. The sun shone in a cloudless sky and it was so hot that some children were wearing summer uniform already. A few mounds of dirty slush beside the road and streaks of white against the hedge-banks were the only visible reminders of the snowy Easter eight days ago.

Here we go again, thought Katy as she sat down in her usual seat, left hand side, third row from the front. Get on the bus, get off, lessons, break, lessons, lunch, lessons, get on the bus, get off – that was her school day. She didn't exactly hate school, but she didn't like it much either. If school were a colour, it would be grey.

Unexpectedly, the bus stopped after about five minutes at the end of the Stonyford Farm track. Three children got on: a tall girl with long fair hair, and two smaller boys with fair hair who looked like identical twins.

To Katy's amazement, the girl stopped by her seat. "Are you saving the other seat for anyone, or can I sit here?" she asked in a confident, rather posh voice.

"Y-yes," stammered Katy in surprise. "I mean yes, do sit here if you like."

For the rest of the journey, the two of them talked without stopping. The girl told Katy that her name was Alice Gardner. Her mum and dad had just got divorced, and Alice, her mum and twin brothers had moved to Stonyford, a farmhouse only a short distance across the moor from Barton Farm. Alice's father was a stockbroker in London, but they had all lived in Surrey. Her mum had owned a riding school there, and she planned to turn Stonyford into a trekking centre. Alice loved riding, owned two ponies called Bella and Shannon, and had already joined the local Pony Club.

Katy told Alice about the farm and her family, including Granfer and Auntie Rachel. Most important of all was the story of the Exmoor filly and how it would be Katy's in the autumn.

In no time at all the bus was pulling up at the school gates. Katy's heart sank. Now Alice would discover she'd accidentally befriended a nobody, and she would pal up with some of the more popular children.

"Can I stick with you for a while?" Alice asked as they got off the bus. "Just till I get to know where everything is?"

"Fine by me," said Katy, and led the way into school.

They'd arrived early, so there was plenty of time to show Alice the most important places: cloakroom, classroom, dining room, staff room, computer room, sports hall and loos.

"It's all so different from my old school," said Alice. "Thank goodness I've got you!" She linked her arm through Katy's as they walked back to their classroom.

Katy noticed several children staring at her glamorous new-found friend, and couldn't help smiling.

They sat together for assembly, maths and geography. Then it was break, and they rushed out into the sunny playground with everyone else.

Claire, one of the super-cool set, came bounding up. "Ali! We met at the Pony Club team trials last week, remember?"

"Of course!" Alice exclaimed. "What a surprise!"

Claire hugged her. "This is *brill*! I didn't realise you were coming here. Come and meet everyone!" She grabbed Alice's hand and pulled her towards the corner of the playground where she and her friends always hung out.

Katy was left standing alone, wondering whether she'd become invisible. Then she noticed a group of girls looking at her, and wished she had.

It was obvious that Alice had been welcomed with open arms by Claire's friends, so Katy kept her distance and made out she didn't care. Several times that day Alice beckoned at her to join them, but she pretended she hadn't seen.

When it was time for the bus home, Alice was already sandwiched between some girls in the back seat when Katy climbed aboard to sit by herself in her usual place. She could hear them comparing mobile phones.

They stopped at the Stonyford lane. Alice made her way to the exit amidst calls from the back of "See you, Ali!" and "Text me!" As she passed Katy, she said, "Bye, Katy. See you tomorrow."

"Bye, Alice. See you," Katy said. But it was too late, she'd got off the bus.

*

That first day set the pattern for the next few weeks. Katy see-sawed between being happy and miserable, and it largely depended on whether Alice was with her or someone else. The trouble was that everyone liked Alice and wanted to be friends with her.

I'm not surprised Alice likes being one of the good-looking, popular set, Katy often thought gloomily. Why am I so short when most of the other girls in the class seem to be getting taller by the day? And why don't I have the kind of hair which can be put into lots of different styles? I can't seem to do anything interesting with my boring brown-ish, long-ish, curly-ish hair.

On the day before half term Katy pretended, as usual, to be looking out of the window at something when the bus stopped at the Stonyford turning. The girls at the back were calling, "Ali! Here! We've saved you a seat, Ali!", so Katy was taken by surprise when Alice sat down next to her.

"Why are you avoiding me all the time? I thought we were supposed to be friends," Alice said bluntly.

Katy was caught off guard. "We are, but . . . but we needn't be friends if you don't want to be. I mean, you've got so many friends now, haven't you? I know you try to be kind – thanks for picking me for your netball team yesterday, by the way – but you really needn't bother. I understand. It's okay, honestly it is."

Alice laughed. "You're such a numpty, Katy!"

"A *whaty*?"

"A numpty! My mum always tells us we're being numpties when we're being silly, and you're being a prize numpty! If it were an Olympic sport you'd win the gold medal, no problem. Can't you see? I *want* to be friends with you!"

"But what about Claire and everyone?"

"I like them too, but it's you I really get on with, Katy – except when you're being a numpty, of course. I've wanted to be your best friend ever since the beginning of term, but you don't seem to like me anymore."

"Of course I like you! I just didn't want you to feel you *had* to be my friend, that's all," Katy said.

Alice hugged her. "Best friends, then?"

Katy nodded happily.

"Brill! With Barton and Stonyford being so close, we'll be able to go riding together and everything!"

Katy came down to earth with a bump. "But I can't ride," she said.

"Well, we'll have to do something about that as quickly as possible then, won't we?" Alice declared. "Misty will teach you!"

"Who's Misty?"

"He's the oldest, wisest pony in the world."

4

Learning to Ride

A lice wasn't the only big change in Katy's life
that summer. Since Gran, Granfer and Rachel
had moved out of Barton Farm, there were three
spare bedrooms and two spare bathrooms in the old
farmhouse. Katy's parents decided to take in bed and
breakfast guests to make up for the lack of income from
the farm.

Katy had mixed feelings about the changes. Mum
now had to spend most of her time cooking, cleaning
and entertaining. This meant that Katy was no longer
alone in the house and they had really good meals

because of the guests. It was fun showing people round the farm as well, and it made Katy really appreciate where she lived for the first time. However, it was very odd having strangers in her home, and a real bore to have to be quiet, well-behaved and tidy all the time.

Alice's mum was very busy too, with three children to look after and a great deal of work to be done if the Stonyford Riding Stables was going to be ready by the beginning of the summer holidays.

True to her word, Alice made sure Katy started learning how to ride as quickly as possible, with the help of her mum, Melanie. "As quickly as possible" turned out to be four o'clock on the first Sunday of the summer half term. It was a moment Katy never forgot.

Misty had kind eyes, a slightly saggy body and a speckled grey coat which shed hairs all over Katy's clothes.

"You needn't worry, he'll look after you. He's a 'been there, done that, got the T-shirt' sort of pony," Melanie said as she held him for Katy to get on from the mounting block. "Well done for sitting on the saddle gently. Misty likes considerate riders, don't you old boy?" She gave Misty an affectionate rub under his mane. "Now then, stirrups on the ball of your foot, like so. Hold one rein in each hand, thumbs on top, that's right, and if you feel unsafe grab hold of the front of the saddle – don't pull on the reins to steady yourself. All you need is a light contact, just to let him know you're there. He's got a very good mouth, considering so many people have learned to ride on him."

Katy wondered what a good mouth was, but was too shy to ask. Later she discovered it meant his mouth was very sensitive and he was obedient to the slightest pressure from the reins.

To be perched on top of a living, breathing pony, and for that pony to seem quite happy about the fact, struck Katy as a miracle. Yet at the same time it felt like the most natural thing in the world to be sitting on Misty, with a neat grey mane running up the slim neck in front of her and two pointed grey ears at the end.

That night, she dreamed she was riding again. But this time the pony's neck in front of her was brown and sturdy, with a bushy mane tumbling down on each side. The pony's short brown ears with black tips were pricked as they galloped over the heather together, barely touching the ground. She was riding her Exmoor pony, and her memory of it was so strong that it was hard to believe it was only a dream.

By the end of half term, having ridden every day, Katy was confident enough to go out on a quiet hack.

Melanie rode her chestnut hunter called Max and led Katy on Misty, while Alice pranced along behind on Shannon.

"Shannon doesn't know the meaning of quiet hack!" Alice laughed as her pony shied at a drain cover by the side of the road and then started jogging sideways, tossing her head impatiently. Alice seemed totally at ease.

I'd love to be that good at riding, Katy thought. Thank goodness Misty's so well-behaved!

"You're a natural, Katy," said Melanie as they trotted back along the farm track. "Would you like to carry on with some lessons after school next week, or at weekends, perhaps, if that would be easier?"

"Oh, I'd love that, but I'm afraid Mum and Dad haven't got enough money at the moment," Katy replied.

"Honestly, don't worry about the money," Melanie said. "You've worked so hard this week that you've earned your lessons. All the tack's gleaming, thanks to you."

"But that wasn't work!" Katy said. It had been brilliant chatting to Alice, cleaning tack and listening to the radio in the sunny stable yard. They'd had a lovely time taking the bridles apart, cleaning all the pieces and putting them back together again – like doing a jigsaw puzzle with a purpose. She added, "In fact, anything to do with horses isn't real work, is it? It's too much fun to be called work."

Melanie laughed. "You're a true horsewoman!" she said.

Katy thought that was one of the nicest things anyone had ever said to her.

Although Misty would always have a special place in Katy's heart, by the summer holidays she was ready to move on to a faster pony for cantering and jumping lessons. She still rode Misty out on hacks with Alice over the moors though, because he was so safe that Melanie could allow the girls to go exploring without her.

For jumping lessons, Melanie let Katy ride a new pony called Jacko. He was a lovely sort of chocolate colour, with a milk chocolate body and a darker chocolate mane and tail. Alice said the proper name for that colour was liver chestnut, but Katy thought chocolate sounded much nicer. Jacko was larger and faster than Misty, a bit like going from a little bike with stabilisers to a top-of-the-range mountain bike with lots of gears. As soon as Katy sat on Jacko she could feel the immense power beneath her. She could also sense something else – a sort of instant connection with him – like she'd felt with the filly on the moor, and with Alice too.

Jacko seemed to love life. He was what Melanie called 'forward-going', and that meant acceleration was pretty easy! All Katy had to do to go faster was lean forward slightly and squeeze gently with her legs. And to go over a jump all she had to do was ride towards it – Jacko did the rest, ears pricked, literally jumping for joy. It felt like flying. Stopping him was sometimes tricky, but as the summer progressed she became better at it. However, to be on the safe side, Melanie didn't let her ride him in wide open spaces. Katy knew she had the best of both worlds, with dependable old Misty for carefree hacks with Alice and wonderful, exciting Jacko for lessons.

Riding, Katy decided, was the best feeling in the world.

5

Branding Time

The weeks sped by, and in no time at all it was autumn.

One night at teatime Dad said, "I got a letter from the Exmoor Pony Society this morning, Sally. They're coming here next Wednesday afternoon for the branding, if that's okay."

"I expect that'll be all right," said Mum. "Better get it over and done with before the house is full of guests for half term. Any idea how many people there'll be for tea?"

"As usual, I have no idea." Dad started to count on

his fingers. "There'll be the secretary, two inspectors, the vet, Mark, Tom, my dad, myself, and I'll see if the Rawle brothers can come and give a hand. That's ten before you account for any buyers or TV crews who may turn up, although rumour has it that buyers are very thin on the ground this year. Sign of the times, I'm afraid."

"Can I have a day off school?" asked Katy excitedly.

"No!" both parents said together.

After school the next day, Katy went up to the moor to see if she could see the ponies. She felt rather guilty that, with all the excitement of riding at Stonyford, she'd neglected her filly. She knew that the ponies could survive perfectly well without her, but she really had meant to go and see her foal much more often. Mostly, she'd seen the ponies when out riding with Alice. They'd been able to get much closer to them on horseback than they could on foot, although they'd had to keep an eye out for Rifle, the stallion. Even steady old Misty had turned and galloped off, with Katy clinging on for dear life, when Rifle had come cantering up, ears back and neck snaking from side to side!

Katy reached the Common gate and, to her amazement, the whole herd was just on the other side.

The ponies appeared to take no notice of her, although they knew she was there. It was as if the gate were a safety barrier.

Before long Katy had picked out her pony. She was grazing with two other foals, looking at Katy out of the corner of her eye. Eventually the filly's curiosity seemed to get the better of her, and she left the others and came up to the gate hesitantly. She was 'mouthing', just like foals do to older horses as a sign of submission. Katy lowered her eyes and tried to make her body as relaxed as she could, although she couldn't stop her heart from racing. The filly walked right up to the gate and started to rub her head against the bars.

Very slowly, Katy worked her way along the gate, shifting her hand along its bars until she was right by the pony's head. Then, very gently, she touched the pony's forehead. A thrill ran up her arm, like a mild electric shock. The foal jumped slightly, as if she had felt the same thing, but she didn't run away.

The two of them stood like that for a few seconds, with Katy gently rubbing her pony's head and talking to her softly. Then the filly decided to turn and trot back to the herd, as if nothing unusual had happened.

Overjoyed, Katy ran back home and found Granfer mending the yard fence. "Guess what,

Granfer," she said breathlessly. "The whole herd's by the Common gate, and I managed to touch my pony!" She'd thought of a name for the filly, but she was planning to keep it a secret until the registration documents were filled in after branding.

"Well done, my girl!" Granfer said, grinning at her. "I think we'd better get those ponies into Moor Field before they disappear over the other side of the Common again, don't you?"

So Katy and Granfer had the easiest pony roundup on record. They just opened the gate and the ponies streamed through: twenty-one mares, five yearlings, nineteen foals and one stallion. Their heads were soon down, eating the sweet, lush cultivated grasses in the field.

"Forty-five, forty-six. Good, they're all here. Isn't that the prettiest sight in the world, Katy?" asked Granfer, as they stood looking at the ponies grazing in the evening sun. The sun made their coats shine and picked out all the different shades, from silvery gold to black and all the brown colours in-between.

"Beautiful, Granfer," she agreed, slipping her hand into his.

"When it comes to ponies choosing between freedom and good food, good food wins every time!" Granfer chuckled.

Every day between then and branding, Katy walked

up to the field to see the ponies, but she didn't manage to touch the filly again.

On the night before branding, the last thing Katy thought before she went to sleep was: *This time tomorrow I'll have a pony of my own.*

B randing day was damp, with a mist like tiny rain drops that seemed to penetrate everywhere and make everything saturated. This type of weather was very common, and was known locally as "raining mud", because everything became muddy in next to no time.

The ponies looked very bedraggled, standing in the back yard with a cloud of steam rising from their bodies.

A couple of prospective buyers had turned up with horse-boxes and there were a few keen members of the Exmoor Pony Society who'd come along out of interest because the Barton herd was so well thought of. There was also a man who was making a video titled *Exmoor Characters*. He wanted to interview Granfer about his lifelong involvement with Exmoor ponies. Granfer was the centre of attention, and he loved it.

In contrast, Katy's dad always dreaded branding day. He'd never got over his childhood fear of ponies, but he wasn't going to tell his father that. Another embarrassment was that he could never tell which pony was which, whereas Granfer could recognise each one and memorise every pedigree for generations.

Each foal had to be separated from its mother. Then it had to be caught and held for inspection, microchipping and branding. This was not a job for the faint-hearted, as the foals had never been handled before and, clearly terrified, they often fought as if their lives depended on it. Microchipping was a relatively new requirement for all foals of any breed. A small microchip was inserted by the vet into the gristle near the top of each foal's neck. Each one had a unique number which would stay with the pony for life and could be read using a hand-held electronic reader. The number was recorded on the foal's passport too. In theory, microchipping meant that branding was no longer needed because each pony could be identified electronically, but at Barton they still branded their ponies as well because they were free-living on the moor. It was relatively simple to read a pony's brand, even from a distance, but to read its microchip you had to catch it, hold it still and stand close – not so easy with a wild Exmoor pony.

The registered ponies all had to be given names as well. Granfer had traditionally named his ponies after wild plants. However, in recent years the choice had been left to his grandchildren. Tom had chosen types of guns and machinery, which was why the herd stallion was Rifle. In contrast, Katy had called the yearling fillies Fudge, Sherbet, Toffee, Ice Cream and Cheesecake, because she loved sweets and puddings.

The filly foals were destined to stay in the Barton herd or be sold on privately, but the colt foals would be sold at Brendon pony sale the following Monday. The sale always coincided with autumn half term, and for many local children it was the highlight of their holiday.

One by one each foal was separated from its mother and the brand number of the mother was recorded. Then the foal was caught and held still, a hair sample was taken for genetic testing and it was inspected to check that all its characteristics were typical of an Exmoor pony.

The inspectors examined each foal carefully, checking for faults like white marks or an unbalanced jaw. It was quite rare for a Barton foal to fail its inspection, but it happened occasionally.

It happened to Katy's filly.

"Some white hairs on the tail here, Geoff," Alan Tucker remarked to his fellow inspector.

"Mmm, I see what you mean, Alan. Could be where another pony's taken a bite at her rump and left a mark, but you can't be too careful. Pity though, it's a cracking filly otherwise."

"What do you think then, Geoff? Inspect her again next year?"

"Yep. That would be the fairest thing, I think."

"Okay. Let her go."

And that was how Katy's pony failed.

B y the time Katy came home from school, everyone was having tea in the kitchen.

"What number is she? I've thought of a name for her!" said Katy excitedly, as she dropped her school bag on the floor and took a sandwich from the table.

"Um . . . Katy, love," said Granfer, eyeing Dad as he spoke. "I'm afraid that pony you wanted failed her inspection, but your dad and I have agreed that you can have the pick of the other fillies instead. Also, you'd better name the others so that Mr Wright can register them."

Katy looked in complete horror at the group of people gathered in the kitchen, eating and drinking as if nothing terrible had happened. They were out of focus and she felt sick. She dropped her half-eaten sandwich and ran upstairs. It was only when she was in the privacy of her room with the door locked behind her that she allowed herself to cry. She cried like she'd never cried before: great heaving sobs from the centre of her body.

She'd believed that she and the filly shared not only a birthday but a common destiny. All her hopes for the future had been built up around the assumption that, from that day on, the two of them would become inseparable. As in a good story, they would walk off into the sunset and live happily ever after. Now everything had gone completely, horribly wrong, and there was nothing she could do about it. She knew her father wouldn't give in about the deal. As far as he was concerned, one Exmoor pony was much the same as any other, but an unregistered one was worse than useless, and Granfer certainly wouldn't have an unregistered Exmoor on the farm. Katy had to admit that half her daydreams had centred around entering, and winning, all the Exmoor pony classes at shows, but unregistered ponies couldn't be shown in Exmoor pony classes.

Her dreams were well and truly shattered.

Down in the kitchen, the tea guests had left. Dad and Granfer were talking and helping Mum with the washing up.

"How about letting Katy keep the filly and getting it inspected again next year?" suggested Granfer. "I'm sure those white hairs are a bite mark. Rifle hasn't sired any foals with white on and Tormentil has never had a foal of hers fail before today. It's just bad luck."

"Don't get me wrong," replied Dad. "I'm just as upset as you are. But you know as well as I do that it's better to take first loss. If the pony fails again next year she won't get any more chances. It'll be much harder to get Katy to part with her after a year than it will be now. As a matter of fact, she hardly took any notice of the Exmoors all summer because she was so wrapped up in her riding lessons. You wait and see, in a couple of weeks she'll have forgotten all about it."

"I hate to admit it, but you're probably right, Phil," Granfer agreed. "To tell the truth, I had my reservations about Katy having a wild pony, and she'd have grown out of that filly before it was old enough to be useful, most likely. Peggy and I have a bit of money put by, and it would be nice to buy our Katy a well-mannered, experienced pony – something she can have a bit of fun on now. We bought Tom his first trials bike when he was about the same age, so it would be fair to buy Katy a pony. What d'you think?"

"Well, if you're sure you can afford it, that would be great. I'd be a good deal happier about that."

"So would I," added Mum. "It'll be much better for Katy to have a safe, fully trained pony that she can look after by herself. I'm sure she'll be thrilled."

Katy was not thrilled.

6

Brendon Pony Sale

The ponies were frightened and confused as they clattered down the steep ramp of the lorry into a holding pen at the sale grounds: eleven colt foals, six old mares and the filly.

Their world had been the Common and Barton Farm, but suddenly everything had changed. They'd been cramped together on a terrifying lorry ride to this noisy, crowded, bewildering place where everything was scary.

Most of the foals had the added stress of being parted from their mothers, and they tried to suckle the old mares for comfort. The mares were thoroughly fed up with this, and had resorted to biting and kicking any foal who approached their flanks.

To add to the misery, it was pouring with rain.

Things were pretty grim for Katy too. She lay on her bed, weighed down by a desperate, crushing sadness, and listened to the rain beating against her window.

Since branding day she'd avoided seeing any of the ponies. It was easier to pretend they didn't exist. Now she felt terribly guilty that she hadn't even said goodbye to her filly. She felt she'd somehow broken a secret promise of trust and friendship that had passed between them at the Common gate a week ago.

"What right have humans to make these stupid rules, anyway?" Katy mumbled tearfully into her pillow. "How would that inspector like to be condemned as useless because he's got a few white hairs?"

She'd said this to Granfer a couple of nights ago, and he'd tried to explain the importance of keeping a breed as special as the Exmoor pony pure and completely true to type, but she hadn't wanted to listen. That was the night Granfer had offered to buy her a "proper" pony. She'd told him in no uncertain terms that if she couldn't have the filly she didn't want anything. Now she might have blown her chances of ever owning a pony, and she'd been very rude and ungrateful – yet another thing to feel guilty about.

On impulse, she fetched her money box, emptied it onto the bed and counted her savings. If only she hadn't spent that money on sweets and a silly make-up set! Would £27.90 be enough?

Katy ran downstairs calling, "Mum! Mum!"

"What's the matter?" Mum asked, rushing out of the kitchen.

"Nothing's the matter, but could you take me to Brendon?"

"Katy, you know I can't, and please don't shout at me. Come and find me if you want to ask me something. I thought something terrible had happened."

"Please, Mum! You can just drop me off and come back."

"No, Katy. I don't want you upsetting yourself over that foal again. Besides, I'm really busy. There'll be five people staying tonight, and I haven't done the rooms yet. If you want to make yourself useful you can go and strip the sheets off the beds for me."

Katy didn't want to make herself useful. She sat on the stairs with her head in her hands, wondering what to do. If Granfer took her to the sale he'd want to stay with her, so that would be no good. Anyway, he never went because he hated seeing his ponies sold. How about walking to Brendon? She'd ridden there and back once in the summer with Melanie and Alice, but it had taken all day. *Melanie and Alice!* Why hadn't she thought of them before? Probably because she knew Alice was staying with her father for the first weekend of half term. But now it was Monday, so she might be back home. It was worth a try.

Mum was working in the kitchen with the radio on. Katy dialled the number for Stonyford. She knew it by heart.

"Hello. Stonyford Riding Stables."

"Alice! Thank goodness you're back! Listen, could your mum take me to Brendon pony sale?"

"Um, I don't know. A group of riders have just cancelled because of the rain, so she may be able to. Just a mo, I'll ask her. Are you sure you want to go though, with the filly there and everything?"

"That's exactly why I want to go! I'm going to buy her!"

"*Buy* her?" Alice exclaimed. "You must be nuts! Your dad will go ballistic, won't he?"

Katy had to admit that she hadn't thought about that. "It's a chance I've got to take," she said grandly.

Alice giggled. "Hang on, I'll ask Mum. She's just outside."

"Don't tell her why."

"I'm not stupid, you know. Stay there, I won't be

50

a minute." Alice was several minutes. She came back to the phone out of breath. "Are you still there, Katy? Sorry, Mum was turning the horses out in the field, and I had to run after her. Guess what? She thinks it's a great idea. We'll pick you up in an hour. Is that all right?"

"If you can get here any earlier, please do. I think that the ponies start selling at midday. It's half past ten now, and we'll have to find them and everything."

"Okay, we'll come as soon as poss. Byeee!"

Katy stood at the kitchen door. "I'm going over to Stonyford, Mum. Melanie's picking me up." Well, it was only half a lie.

"That's nice, love. Have a good time," Mum replied with relief. Now she could get on with her work in peace.

Fifty minutes later, Katy, Alice, the twins and Melanie were all driving to Brendon. They arrived just before twelve, and luckily found a parking space in the field behind the pub. The awful weather had put a lot of people off.

"You two girls stick together like glue, then," said Melanie. "Don't talk to strangers, and here's £10 for you to buy something to eat and drink."

"Thanks!" the girls chorused as they rushed down the street to the sale ground. There was a large, flat field where all sorts of things were being sold: gates, pig arcs, bicycles, hens, ferrets, trailers, building supplies, tack, and pretty well anything you could imagine. It looked fascinating, but the girls didn't have time to stop. They went straight on to the pony pens.

A crowd of people were already gathered five deep round the pens. Some horses, including a huge cart horse with enormous hairy legs, stood tied to a wooden fence. The pens were full of wild ponies of different sizes and colours. Some looked like true Exmoors, but most of them weren't.

Where on earth were the Barton ponies? It was much busier than Katy had expected, and she couldn't see a thing. She felt panic rising inside her, but just then she spotted one of the Rawle brothers standing nearby. "Do you know which pen Granfer's ponies are in, Matt?" she asked breathlessly.

"The one in the corner over there, maid. D'you want me to lift you up so you can see?"

"Oh, yes please, but, but I'm rather heavy, I'm afraid."

"Nonsense," said Matt Rawle as he lifted Katy effortlessly onto his broad shoulders. Now she could see everything. There was a round, empty ring in the centre, with pens full of ponies in a semicircle around it. In the far corner there was a dispirited group of Exmoors. They had to be the Barton ponies. Katy panicked again. However hard she tried, she couldn't pick out her filly from the other foals. All their coats were dark with rain, and they were huddled together with their heads hung low, so it was impossible to tell them apart. She couldn't stay up on Matt's shoulders for the whole sale.

"How do they sell the ponies, Matt?" she asked.

"With difficulty," Matt teased. Then he went on a bit more seriously, "The ponies are split into groups, or lots, and as they're brought into the auction ring people bid for them. The person offering the highest price is the poor fool who gets to keep the pony. Ready to come down now? I told your father I'd meet him in the bar for a beer."

"Oh, please don't tell Dad I'm here, Matt!" pleaded Katy. "Just one more question. How do you vote for a pony?"

"It's called bidding, Kate, not voting! Different people bid in different ways. They touch their nose, nod their head or raise their catalogue slightly, for instance. It seems to me there's rather a lot I'd better not tell your dad!"

"Oh, I was just wondering," Katy said as casually as she could.

"Well, bye then. Take my advice – keep your hands firmly in your pockets. If you so much as pick your nose, you may end up with a herd of ponies!" Matt said cheerfully. He lowered Katy to the ground and walked off in the direction of the bar.

It seemed to Katy and Alice that the problem was going to be getting noticed by the auctioneer at all, with such a big crowd between them and the ring.

Clang! Clang Clang! Clang! Clang Clang! A man ringing a hand bell walked by, and even more people flocked to the pony pens. As if on cue, the sun broke through the rain clouds and shone on the scene like a spotlight. Steam rose from the ponies.

"I think that means that they're going to start selling," Alice shouted in Katy's ear.

"Help! What do I do now?" squeaked Katy.

Just then, a large man in front of Katy trod backwards onto her foot.

"So sorry, love," he said. "Why don't you girls squeeze in front of me to that space at the rails there?"

"Thanks very much," they said. Squeeze was the right word. They found it difficult to breathe with so many people pressing in on them, but at least now they had a good view of the sale ring.

"Good afternoon, Ladies and Gentlemen," boomed the auctioneer. "We've a good selection of equines here for you today. We'll start with the wild ones and then move on to the halter broken and ridden ones. Right, we'll start with the ponies from Jack Squires' herd at Barton. These need no introduction, folks. Fine herd of Exmoors, kept on the moor all year round as nature intended. Let's have the mares first please, Bill."

Katy's heart started to race, and she was in a complete panic. She hadn't bargained on the Barton ponies being first, and she needed time to see how to bid.

"Help!" Katy whispered.

"You'll be fine!" Alice whispered back.

"Well, here's a fine bunch of registered Exmoor mares, all full pedigree. Born and raised at Barton Farm. They've bred good foals in the past and have been running with the herd stallion, Barton Rifle. Take your pick or take the lot. Just right for someone wanting to start a herd of their own. Used to fending for themselves on the moor. Who'll start me at £30? Yes! Thank you, Madam: 30 . . . 30 . . . 32 . . . 34 . . . 34 . . . 36 . . . 38 . . . 40 . . . 42 . . . 44 . . . 46, this is more like it, 48 . . . 50 . . . 50 . . . 52 . . ."

Katy looked around, frantically trying to see what signals the bidders were giving, but she couldn't see a thing. The auctioneer was rattling off numbers so fast that she couldn't understand what he was saying for most of the time.

". . . All done, then, at £54!" the auctioneer announced. "You'll take the lot, Madam? And your name? Thank you." He wrote something on his clipboard, then carried on. "What have we now? We'd better take that filly next. She'll panic if she's left in the pen by herself after we've sold the colts."

Katy felt like shouting, "This is unfair! I'm not

ready yet!" Instead, she stood gripping the bars of the auction ring, trying not to faint.

"Oops!" said the auctioneer, as the filly and a colt came careering into the ring. "All right then, leave them both together, but it's the filly we're selling. What's that, Madam? Yes, she's the larger of the two, with a slightly lighter coat, if you can see that. Now apparently she's not branded at present due to a few white baby hairs in her tail, which are bound to grow out by next year when she can be inspected again. As you can see, she's well-grown for her age, and I wouldn't be at all surprised to see her carrying off all the prizes at shows in a few years' time. Impeccable breeding. Who'll start me at £40?"

Katy's heart sank

"£30?"

Still too much.

"Well, start me where you will, then."

Katy wasn't sure what that meant, so she kept quiet.

"£10!" A woman called from somewhere on Katy's right.

"Thank you, Madam. £10 we've got 10 . . . 10 . . . who'll give me 12?"

"Go on! Quick!" Alice hissed in Katy's ear.

"What do I do?"

"Bid more, or that woman will get her."

"I will!" shouted Katy. Everyone turned to look at

her. She could have died of embarrassment. Her cheeks were burning.

"Thank you, Madam," said the auctioneer, barely hiding his amusement.

"12 . . . 14 . . . 14 . . ."

Alice nudged Katy, and Katy raised her arm high above her head, as if she were at school. It worked. The auctioneer smiled and nodded at her.

"16 . . . 18 . . . 18 . . . 20 . . . 22 . . . A first class filly, mind. You won't have the expense of gelding her."

A ripple of laughter spread round the ring.

"22 . . . 24 . . . 24 . . ."

Katy was in a complete panic now. She'd only got £27.90 in her pocket. Why had Granfer said that an un-registered filly was worthless? £24 was a lot of money! Why had she spent her money on silly things like sweets?

". . . 26 . . ."

Please don't go any higher.

". . . 28 . . . 28 . . ."

Well, that was it. She'd lost her.

"All done at £28?" asked the auctioneer.

"Katy!" whispered Alice, handing her the £10 which Melanie had given them for lunch.

Katy's hand shot up.

"Still with us, then?" smiled the auctioneer. ". . . 30 . . . 30 . . ."

"How much have I got?" Katy hissed to Alice.

"£37.90 if you don't mind starving!" Alice replied.

". . . 32 . . . 34. Do I have 36?" asked the auctioneer.

This is like slow torture, Katy thought. I can bid one more time, but if it goes any higher I've lost her for good.

At that moment, the filly stopped trotting round the ring. She stood still, head up, eyes bright and nostrils wide. Steam rose from her quivering muscles as she whinnied in the direction of home with all her might.

Tears prickled Katy's eyes. Blindly, she raised her hand again.

"It's all right, young lady, you needn't bid against yourself," the auctioneer said, smiling at Katy. "Are you out, Madam? Very well. Going once! Going twice! Sold! Sold to? Your name, please, young lady."

Katy opened her mouth to speak, but she could only manage a shaky whisper.

"Sorry, you'll have to speak up a bit."

"Katy Squires from Barton Farm," said Alice, coming to Katy's rescue yet again.

The auctioneer chuckled. "Well, I've seen it all now!" he said. "Does Phil know about this?"

"No," whispered Katy.

"No, he doesn't," said Alice in her loud, confident voice. "We want it to be a surprise."

"It'll be that all right!" the auctioneer guffawed, and everyone laughed with him.

Katy and Alice wriggled out of the crowd. When they had room to breathe, they turned to each other, clapped hands and shouted, "YES!"

"What do we do now?" asked Katy, suddenly becoming serious.

"Go and pay the people in the shed over there. Then find Mum, and hope she's in a good mood," said Alice.

Katy's dad bought a set of chain harrows and a box of old tools in the implement sale, then he spent the rest of the day drinking with his friends in the bar. He certainly wasn't interested in watching the ponies being sold. He felt rotten about Katy's filly and didn't want to see her sold for meat, which was the most probable destiny for an unregistered wild pony.

"Jack's mares have just made £54 apiece, Phil," said Matt Rawle as he joined him at the bar.

"Looks like the drinks are on me, then. What are they selling now?"

"That filly your daughter's taken a fancy to."

"Oh, no. I can't tell you how bad I feel about it, Matt. I should never have made that silly deal with Katy. I suppose there's just a chance it'll go to a good home nearby."

"I expect there's every possibility it might just end up in a home-from-home," Matt said, smiling.

"The trouble is," Dad said, "who in their right mind would buy a wild, unregistered Exmoor foal?"

"Oh, I can think of one or two people – well – one, anyway."

"I do hope you're right," Dad replied. "I wonder what everybody's finding so amusing out there. I hope the filly hasn't escaped."

"Depends what sort of a filly you mean," Matt chortled as he drained his glass.

"What?"

"Oh, nothing. My round. Same again?"

After all the horses and ponies had been sold, the auctioneer went into the bar for a well-earned drink.

"How did the ponies sell, Hugh?" Dad asked the auctioneer.

"Yours better than most, Phil, but that isn't saying much, I'm afraid."

"And the filly? Please tell me that a nice lady with a kind face bought her."

"Don't you worry yourself, Phil. I've just seen a very nice lady loading that filly into a very smart horse-box."

"Was the buyer local, then?" Dad asked.

"Very," the auctioneer replied.

Everyone in the bar collapsed with laughter.

7

Winter at Stonyford

It was only when they were driving home, with Katy's precious cargo in the horse-box behind them, that the enormity of what she'd done hit Katy.

"Do you think Trifle will be lonely all by herself?" she asked Melanie anxiously.

"*Trifle!* Is that really what you're going to call her?" Alice exclaimed.

"Yes. I've had it planned for months. It's rather clever, actually," Katy replied in hurt tones. She thought it was a brilliant name.

"How come it's so clever, then?" asked Alice. She

could be annoyingly superior sometimes.

"Her mum was called Tormentil and her dad was called Rifle, so if you mix the two words you get Trifle. Also, it happens to be one of my favourite puddings."

"Well, I think it's a very good name," said Melanie diplomatically. "And in answer to your question, Katy, she probably will be lonely for a while, but she'll get used to it if you give her plenty of attention and she has sheep or cattle for company. Ponies do like to be with their own kind, but a lot of them seem to survive quite happily by themselves. Also, if she's looking to you for friendship she'll be easier to handle, I expect."

"I don't know if Dad will let me put her with the sheep and cows. I remember him saying that ponies get ill if they eat cattle and sheep cake because they have different kinds of tummies. To tell the truth, I haven't really thought about where I'm going to keep her or anything," Katy said miserably.

"How about keeping her at Stonyford for the winter? It would be quite a help to me actually. She could be company for Jessie's foal when I wean her this week," Melanie replied. "You could do a bit of work at weekends and in the Christmas holidays to pay for her keep."

"Oh, thank you so much, Melanie! That would be brilliant!" Katy exclaimed.

*

For the rest of the winter term, Katy spent every spare moment at Stonyford. She made herself as useful as possible, mucking out, cleaning tack and even helping in the house. In return she had riding lessons on Jacko, and Trifle had a good home for the winter.

Taming Trifle was much more difficult than Katy had expected. At first the young pony was obviously terrified of all humans. Perhaps being weaned from her mother, followed by bad experiences at the pony sale, had taught her that humans were not to be trusted. Katy couldn't get near her. It seemed their special bond had been destroyed, or perhaps it had never really existed.

Katy wondered if she would ever get a head collar on Trifle, let alone ride her one day.

"I should leave Trifle to settle in for a while before you start handling her. Rome wasn't built in a day, remember," Melanie said one afternoon when they were discussing Trifle while cleaning tack.

"That's one of Mum's favourite sayings," Alice said, smiling at Katy's puzzled face. "It means important work takes time, or something like that."

"But Granfer told me that when he used to tame ponies every year he'd get head collars on the foals straight after they were weaned. He always says you should start handling them as soon as possible."

"Why don't you ask Granfer for some advice,

then?" Melanie suggested. "I'm sure he'd love to help you."

O f course, Katy couldn't ask Granfer to help her because, unknown to Melanie, he didn't know she'd bought Trifle. She desperately wanted his advice, but she knew she'd have to be careful not to give her secret away.

The opportunity arose one rainy Sunday afternoon. Katy was doing her homework on the farm computer in the corner of the kitchen when Granfer came in to make himself a cup of tea.

"Granfer? When you broke in ponies, how did you get them to stop being afraid of you?" she asked, hoping she'd made the question sound unimportant.

Granfer replied enthusiastically. "That can be one of the most difficult things to get right, Katy. There's a knack to it, which only some people have. If you're bossy, impatient or nervous you won't stand a chance. The pony mustn't be afraid of you but he must respect you. It's a tricky balance."

"But how do you actually *do* that?" Katy asked earnestly.

"Well, the way my father taught me was this, and it's worked well for me," Granfer replied as he sat down at the table, warming his hands around a steaming mug of tea. "You keep the pony in a stall by himself with some hay but no water. The only company the pony gets is your company, and the only water he gets is when you give it to him. To begin with he'll be terrified each time you enter the stable and he won't eat or drink when you're there, but pretty soon he'll look forward to you visiting because he's lonely and thirsty and you are his one source of comfort. Gradually you'll be able to get closer to him, and eventually you'll be able to touch him, but you have to be patient. Treats in a bucket like oats or apples help too, but in my opinion it's best not to give titbits by hand – it can teach a pony to bite."

Katy didn't like the idea of locking Trifle up without any water or company, even if it did make her pony want to see her. Besides, there wasn't a spare stable at Stonyford. Trifle had to stay out in the field, as company for Jessie foal, Promise. "Doesn't Auntie Rachel have a special way of breaking in horses?" she asked. "I'm sure I've heard her talk about it."

"Yes, I think she calls it natural horsemanship, but more fanciful people call it horse whispering. It seems to be the fashion nowadays. I'm in two minds about it, myself. These so-called whisperers claim to have invented it all, but on the whole they're doing what horsemen have been doing for generations, as far as I can see. Basically, they've learned how to use that horse language I was telling you about. Some people, like Rachel, have got it down to a fine art, though, and they get tremendous results using it. You ought to ask her about it, really." He looked at her over his steamed-up spectacles. "Any reason why you're so interested all of a sudden?" he asked.

Katy blushed bright red. She really hated lying, especially to Granfer. "No, not really," she said.

As soon as Granfer had gone out of the kitchen, Katy looked up horse whispering on the computer. There was a bewildering amount of information on the subject, including advertisements for expensive courses, but none of the websites gave her what she needed: a simple step-by-step guide to taming Trifle.

That night Katy lay awake in bed, listening to the wind rattling the slates on the roof and wondering how on earth she was going to catch her pony and start training her. I can't ask Rachel for advice in case she guesses about Trifle, she thought. Her half-awake mind wandered to Trifle as a newborn foal, and how she'd instinctively come up to Katy . . . how it had felt so right . . . how being with Alice had felt so easy from the first time she'd met her . . . how riding Jacko had felt so natural from the first time she'd sat on his back. Trust my instincts, do what feels right, she thought sleepily.

So Katy trusted her instincts and did what felt right with Trifle, and it seemed to work – most of the time, one way or another.

And when things didn't go according to plan, Alice kept her spirits up. "Remember, Rome wasn't built in a day!" she'd say in a funny voice, and they'd both end up laughing.

In fact, they said it so much that it became a sort of motto.

For the first couple of weeks, Katy spent the brief period of daylight after school, and longer at weekends, in Trifle's field. She tried to take no notice of her pony. Instead, she just wandered around the field or made a fuss of Promise, who'd been handled from birth and was very friendly. As planned, Trifle became inquisitive, especially when she saw how much Promise liked Katy's company, and every day she dared to come a little closer.

On a cold, wet Thursday evening in the middle of November, something wonderful happened. Katy was giving Promise a goodnight hug over the gate when she felt something brush against her hands on the other side of the young horse's neck. A gush of warm breath followed, and then the more definite feeling of Trifle's soft muzzle on her hands. She'd touched Trifle! No, it was even better than that – Trifle had touched *her*!

From then on, Katy managed to touch Trifle every day, sometimes briefly and sometimes for longer. However, it always seemed to be on Trifle's terms – she decided when to come, when to stand still and when to move away. Katy knew the next stage had to be the head collar, but getting it onto her pony's head was going to be easier said than done.

Both Trifle and Promise were being fed pony nuts in a bucket twice a day, and that gave Katy an idea. She waited until the weekend, so she'd have plenty of time if she needed it, and then tried out her plan.

Armed with two feed buckets and a pony-sized head collar, she entered the field. She had a lead rope with a clip at one end tied around her waist. Trifle and Promise cantered over, by now aware that buckets meant food.

Trifle shoved her nose eagerly into the bucket, oblivious to the fact that on the way she'd put her nose into the head collar.

With slow, sure movements, Katy looped the long strap behind Trifle's ears and did up the buckle.

Trifle munched away, apparently unaware of what was going on.

I've done it! Katy thought, resisting the urge to

jump up and down with excitement. Why is it that things you think are going to be difficult often turn out to be easy, and things which should be easy turn out to be difficult?

Full of confidence now, she untied the lead rope from her waist, reached into the bucket and, fumbling a little, clipped it to the ring behind the nosepiece of the headcollar – *snap!*

The noise of the clip made Trifle jump. Her head shot up and the bucket came with it, lodging over her head like a helmet. The remains of the pony nuts cascaded down over her face. Blinded by the bucket and terrified beyond reason, she spun round, pulling the rope from Katy's hand, and charged round the field. Promise – thinking it was a great game – galloped off in hot pursuit, bucking and leaping.

Katy stood, petrified, wondering which of several potential disasters would happen first. Trifle and Promise were both going to get terribly hurt, and it would all be her fault. "Steady! Whoa!" she pleaded over and over, even though it seemed pointless.

Trifle slowed to a high-stepping trot, turning her head this way and that, trying to get her bearings, still with the bucket over her eyes and the lead rope dragging along the ground.

This would be funny if it wasn't so serious, Katy thought. "Steady! Steady, Trifle!" she said, trying to be soothing even though her voice was shaking.

Trifle slowed to a walk, turned towards Katy and came up to her. She stood, quivering.

Promise carried on around the field, hoping the fun wouldn't stop.

Talking in a low, calm voice, Katy eased the bucket from Trifle's head. As it came off, the pony snorted and backed away. Katy breathed a sigh of relief, walked over to the fence and put the bucket safely on the other side. She turned back, and there was Trifle right behind her!

Has she followed me because she thinks there's still food in the bucket? Katy wondered. Gently, she took hold of the lead rope and walked towards the gate. Trifle followed. At the gate, Katy carefully unclipped the lead rope, stroked her pony, opened the gate, went through, and closed it.

Trifle stood there, her chin resting on the top bar.

Katy stroked her fluffy neck and said softly, "You are a numpty! Wasn't it lucky I was there to save you from that scary bucket-hat?" She smiled to herself. "In a funny sort of way, I think we may have built a little bit of Rome today, Trifle. What d'you think?"

By the Christmas holidays, Trifle would come to the gate when she was called, lead quite well and pick up her feet when asked. She loved being groomed, too.

"You've done wonders with that pony," Melanie commented as Katy led Trifle round the stable yard, followed by Alice leading Promise. "Your grandfather's training methods obviously work."

"Oh, but I didn't do what he suggested," said Katy.

"Really? What method did you use?" asked Melanie.

"The 'Rome wasn't built in a day' method," Alice chipped in, and they all laughed.

As the girls put Trifle and Promise back in the field, Katy said, "Wouldn't it be great if ponies could talk to each other like we do? Then we wouldn't have to train them at all. We could just put a good pony, like Misty, in with an unbroken one, like Trifle, and the job would be done."

"Hmm. What if Trifle taught Misty to be naughty instead? Ponies could pass on tips about the best way to buck people off and things like that!" Alice replied.

"True. I didn't think of that."

As if to prove Alice right, Trifle and Promise took one look at each other and galloped across the field, leaping and squealing.

The two girls laughed as they watched them go.

On a clear, sunny day just before Christmas, Katy went for a hack on Jacko with Melanie on Max.

and Alice on Bella. Jacko had been clipped the day before. His sleek new appearance made him look like a mini racehorse. He felt a bit like one too, as they trotted briskly up the steep lane between Stonyford and the Common. The sound of horseshoes on tarmac rang out in the still air.

Jacko pounded up the hill behind Max, ears pricked forwards, neat brown mane bouncing with each long stride. His enthusiasm for life always made her feel happy all over, and she couldn't help grinning.

At the brow of the hill, Melanie slowed her horse to a walk and then halted by the gate onto the Common. "Would you like to try Jacko on the Common, Katy?" she asked. "See how it goes?"

Katy felt a flutter of excitement in her stomach. "Yes please!" she said.

They went through the gate and out onto the Common. Katy was ready for Jacko to get wound up as soon as his feet touched the moorland, but his mood didn't seem to change at all.

"This way," said Melanie.

They followed her at a walk along a sheep track, into a shallow valley and up the other side to a broad, heather-clad plateau. There she broke into a trot.

Alice rode up alongside. Katy could feel Jacko quicken his pace and take a hold, keen to keep ahead. Alice grinned and gave her a thumbs up sign.

Katy briefly saw Melanie turn round to look at them both. She seemed to be saying something like "Okay?"

At exactly the same moment, all three horses surged forwards and accelerated, powering up the hill. Jacko was going so fast that Katy couldn't feel his hooves touching the ground at all. Automatically, she leaned forwards, took her weight onto her knees and rested her hands on each side of his glossy neck. Air rushed into her open mouth and she squinted to stop her eyes from watering. Looking down, she saw Jacko's legs pounding away and the mottled moorland whizzing by in a blur beneath her.

We must be galloping, Katy thought, unless horses can go faster than a gallop. The odd thing was that she didn't feel at all frightened. She just felt completely at one with Jacko, as if they had turned into one being, sharing the same thoughts and actions. This is living! This is what life's all about! Katy said to herself as they thundered along.

All too soon, Max slowed down. Jacko and Bella followed suit, and they walked side-by-side, snorting and steaming.

"Okay?" This time there was no mistaking what Melanie had said.

"More than okay!" Katy replied. "Jacko's amazing! He's the best pony ever!"

"He is lovely, isn't he?" Melanie said. "In fact,

I'm afraid he's a bit too good to keep for trekking at Stonyford. He deserves better. What he needs is a nice, knowledgeable, competitive home where he can reach his full potential. I'm planning to keep him until Easter and then I'll advertise him for sale. Ponies always sell better in the spring."

Katy wanted to shout, "No! You can't! I'll do anything you want, but please, please don't sell him!" Instead, she said nothing, but she screamed inside all the way home and for a long time after that.

8

Secrets

Katy really did mean to tell her family about Trifle, but the moment never seemed to be right. The longer she left it, the more difficult it was to tell them.

The situation was complicated even more by the fact that Melanie thought Katy's parents knew all about her purchase. Only Alice knew it was a secret, and the problem of how to tell everyone was a frequent topic of conversation between the two friends.

*

I t was Granfer who found out about Katy's secret.

On a cold, frosty morning in February, he drove into the Stonyford Yard. He parked the car, got out and shook Melanie's hand. "Morning. Lovely day."

"Yes, isn't it wonderful?" Melanie replied. "We could do with a fortnight of this to dry out the ground a bit. I want to put a new surface down on the outdoor school over there."

"Nice to see you've got an Exmoor here," remarked Granfer as he looked over the gate at Trifle grazing in the paddock with Promise. "What herd's she from? She looks as if she could be one of ours, except there's no brand on her."

"Yes, she is. That's Katy's pony, Trifle."

"What, *our* Katy?"

"Yes," said Melanie, giving him a puzzled look. Perhaps he's losing his memory, she thought. "That's the Exmoor Katy bought at Brendon last autumn. You know, the filly that wasn't branded."

"Phil and Sally had no idea about this, and nor did I," Granfer replied. A broad grin spread over his face. "Well, well, well . . . Katy is a dark horse! No wonder she wanted to know about breaking ponies. I came here to give her a surprise, and she's given me one instead!"

"You mean she didn't tell you she'd bought the filly? Oh, I am so sorry! I had the impression that you knew! Although, now I come to think of it, she never actually *said* so."

"Don't apologise," Granfer said. "I'm really rather proud of Katy for going ahead and doing what she thought was right. She's a true Squires, that girl. You seem to have done a good job gentling her," remarked Granfer as he stroked Trifle over the gate.

"Katy's the one who's been training her," said Melanie. "She's spent hours with that pony – loves her to bits. Trifle seems to love her as well. The two of them really do seem to have a special sort of bond."

"May be something to do with Katy seeing the foal so soon after she was born. Imprinting, I think it's called – a bond which forms in the first few hours of life," Granfer said.

"The fact that Trifle wasn't branded must have helped her to trust people, too. I don't like the idea of branding at all."

"You're not alone in that, but in my experience they seem to forget about it very quickly," Granfer replied.

"But surely it's unnecessary now that all foals have to be microchipped?"

"Not entirely. You see, to read a microchip you have to get right up close to the pony and keep it still – not so easy with an unhandled mare in the middle of the moor. The trouble is that all Exmoors have the same look about them, with no white markings or anything, so it's hard to tell them apart without a brand mark," Granfer explained.

"I see the problem," said Melanie. "What do the brands mean, then?"

"The star on the shoulder is the Exmoor Pony Society mark. Underneath that is the herd number, and then the individual number of the pony is on its rump. An exception is that ponies from the Anchor herd have an anchor brand."

"Well, I've certainly learned a lot today," said Melanie.

"So have I!" Granfer replied, looking at Trifle. "Now then, how about a pony that Katy can ride now. Do you know of any for sale that might fit the bill?"

"As a matter of fact, I think I may have just the pony for you," Melanie replied.

Granfer smiled to himself. Typical horse-dealer talk, he thought.

However, a couple of hours later – after he'd inspected the pony and seen it ridden – Granfer had to admit that Melanie was right. If Katy had a pony like that it would last her a long time and give her a lot of fun. The only thing which wasn't perfect was the price. He'd have to cash in some savings, but it would be worth it. He didn't want to give Katy any old pony; he wanted to give her the best he could afford – a pony to be proud of. "Can I make a deal with you?" he asked.

9

A Brilliant Birthday

Katy's birthday present was a well-kept secret. Only Katy's family and Melanie knew about it.

As the Easter holidays loomed, Katy became more and more worried. Melanie now had too many horses and ponies at Stonyford – some for the trekking business and others for schooling or selling – so Katy had agreed to take Trifle home after lambing.

How was she going to tell her parents about her pony? Would she be allowed to keep her? If so, how would Trifle cope with being alone? All these questions haunted Katy.

Her other big dread was that Jacko would be sold and she'd never see him again. Ponies like that were snapped up fast, and Melanie had said last Christmas that she'd sell him in the spring – to a knowledgeable, competitive home where he'd be able to reach his full potential, she'd said.

Well, that rules me out as Jacko's prospective owner, even if I did have the money, which I don't, Katy thought. She had an awful feeling that time was driving her fast towards a brick wall, and on the other side was a life without Trifle or Jacko.

There was nothing she could do about losing Jacko, but she had to do her best to keep Trifle. She made herself a promise: she'd tell her parents about Trifle on her birthday. They might be a bit more understanding then.

Katy woke up on the morning of her birthday with a feeling of dread rather than excitement. She lay in bed for ages, rehearsing what she was going to say to her parents. At lambing time her mum didn't take in guests because she was too busy, but she always cooked a proper breakfast for the family at nine o'clock. That way, Dad had a good meal after his night shift and the rest of the family were set up for he day ahead. Katy had decided breakfast would be the best time to tell them about Trifle.

The smell of frying bacon wafted into Katy's room, accompanied by an unusual amount of noise and laughter from downstairs. Breakfasts during lambing weren't usually a time for witty conversation. Perhaps a neighbour had dropped in, so everyone was making a special effort.

Reluctantly, Katy got out of bed. As she walked along the corridor to the bathroom, she was sure she heard Auntie Rachel's voice, followed by Granfer's, then more laughter. How peculiar. As she padded back to her bedroom, an awful thought struck her: now she'd have to tell Granfer and Rachel about Trifle too!

Katy got dressed as slowly as she could, and crept downstairs. The smell of frying, which she usually found irresistible, turned her stomach.

Everyone stopped talking when she entered the kitchen.

"Happy Birthday, love. Had a good lie-in?" asked Mum.

"Catching up on much-needed beauty sleep?" teased Tom.

Katy punched his shoulder.

"Now, now! Behave yourselves," Mum said automatically.

Dad reached under the kitchen table and pulled out a bulky package wrapped in brown paper which Katy guessed was a bucket. "Happy Birthday, Katy. This is from Mum and me," he said.

Katy unwrapped it. It was a bucket, but it was full to the brim with all the things needed to make up a really good grooming kit. "Thank you! It's got everything in it!" she exclaimed, laying each item carefully on the kitchen table. "Even plaiting bands," she said, noticing wistfully that they were dark chocolate-brown, like Jacko's mane.

Now or never, she thought. "Um, there's something I want . . ."

Granfer quickly interrupted, "We all know what you want, maid! It's outside."

"No, Granfer! You don't understand . . ." Katy desperately tried to continue now she'd found the courage to start.

"Come on, before we all burst from having to keep the secret for so long," said Tom, taking Katy by the hand and dragging her towards the front door.

"It's a secret that I want to tell *you* about," Katy continued. "You see, I bought Trifle from . . ."

"Don't worry, we know all about that – Granfer

told us ages ago!" Tom said.

"*What*? How? I mean . . ."

Tom opened the door with a flourish.

"Trifle! Jacko!" Katy gasped. Had she somehow gone back to sleep rather than going downstairs? This had to be a dream.

Melanie and Alice were standing outside the door, holding Trifle and Jacko by their head collars. Both ponies were very excited about their new surroundings.

"You took your time!" said Alice. "We've been freezing out here!"

Everyone sang *Happy Birthday*.

Katy rubbed her eyes, expecting to wake up at any minute. What on earth was going on? Perhaps it was something to do with April Fool's Day.

When everyone had stopped singing, Granfer took Jacko's lead rope from Alice and gave it to Katy.

"Happy Birthday, Katy. This is your Christmas and birthday present from Gran and me for the next ten years!"

"And the head collars are a present from Mum and me!" Alice added. "Trifle's is a bit big at the moment, but she'll soon grow into it. They're real leather ones, and they cost a fortune – not as much as Jacko, though, he cost a mega-fortune!"

"Alice!" Melanie exclaimed, and everyone laughed.

Katy didn't trust herself to speak in case she burst into tears. She just hugged everybody in turn, including the ponies. She hadn't dreamed such happiness was possible.

10

Last Chance

Sometimes there's a summer that's remembered forever as particularly special. Katy's first summer with Jacko and Trifle was one of those.

Rachel had given Katy membership of the local Pony Club for her birthday present, and the calendar in the kitchen at Barton Farm was soon full of Pony Club events: rallies, outings and fun rides, to name a few.

At first, Katy had been very worried that all the other members would be much better than her. However, although Alice, Claire and a few others were really good riders, several were of a similar standard to Katy. Having Alice as a friend had given her so much self-confidence that it was easy to make friends now, so she didn't mind if Alice was in a different teaching group.

Jacko boosted Katy's confidence, too. He was cheeky and fun, patient and kind, and he taught her more about riding than any instructor could have done. Everyone, especially Katy, loved Jacko.

By the end of the summer holidays, Katy wondered how she'd survived for so long without ponies. Her whole life now seemed to revolve around them.

Another highlight of the holidays was a trip with Granfer to Exford Show, where he was judging some of the pony classes. Alice and Melanie were riding in various competitions, and Auntie Rachel was showing a hunter from the livery yard, so Katy had lots to see and do. Because of Granfer, Katy was treated like a VIP in the Exmoor Pony Society tent, and she loved it. She couldn't help looking at all the cups and rosettes on the trophy table and wondering whether Trifle might win them one day!

At home, Granfer and Katy often went for rides together. He rode the quad bike and she rode Jacko. With Granfer as her guide, Katy discovered a whole new world just beyond the farm.

"See those deer over there, Katy?"

"No, where?"

"You've got to look, maid, and get tuned in. See those thorn trees on the other side of the stream? There are six stags I can see straight off. See the sunlight glinting on their horns?"

"Oh yes! Now I see them! Why didn't I spot them before?"

"Youngsters aren't taught how to look nowadays, that's why. If you memorise exactly how the landscape should be, you'll be able to spot if anything's different. You get a sort of feeling for it if you practice. That big stag on the hill looks as if he's rights three and four."

"What on earth does that mean?" Katy asked.

"When a stag can properly be called a stag, he has 'all his rights', which means he has brow, bay and trey points and two on top on each side. That usually happens at around five years old. Each year after that, until he's about ten, he'll get one more point on each side and his horns will get bigger."

"I thought they were called antlers."

"Well, most Exmoor people call them horns. Just to be different, I suppose." Granfer grinned. "Every stag has unique horns, a bit like humans have unique fingerprints, but of course every year stags shed their horns and grow new ones with a bit more added on. Sometimes the horns develop unevenly, as has happened with that stag. I expect he's seven years old and nearing his prime."

"What are the names of the points again, Granfer?"

"When we get home, I'll draw a picture for you. That's the best way to explain," said Granfer. "Now then, young lady, you've got your reins too short again, haven't you? Forget all that Pony Club stuff about having your pony on the bit or whatever. You're on the moor now, and you must give that pony his head. He needs to put his head down to see where he's going. Let him relax and think for himself. It all comes back to learning to trust each other. He's a generous, sensible sort, and if you allow him to work things out rather than nagging at him the whole time, he'll look after you."

It was all very confusing, Katy thought. People had various ideas about riding, and they all seemed to think their way was the correct one. She'd been taught by a girl at Pony Club who'd constantly told her off for having her reins too long, whereas Melanie had taught her to ride on a longer rein. Granfer seemed to be saying that her reins should only be used in an emergency! Katy said this to Granfer, and he laughed.

"You're absolutely right, you know," he agreed. "There are as many ways of riding as there are riders. What works for one horse and rider doesn't work for another, and everyone has their pet theories. I reckon that as long as your horse works happily and well, it doesn't much matter what you do. I can think of several Exmoor farmers who wouldn't win any prizes in a dressage test, but they leave everyone else standing when it comes to riding fast over difficult country."

"I suppose it's the same with taming wild foals," said Katy. "I mean, people have invented lots of different ways of doing it, and some things work better than others, but nobody can say their method is the best, can they? It depends on the person and the pony, and what feels right, doesn't it?" Katy told Granfer about how she'd tamed Trifle with her "Rome wasn't built in a day" method. He laughed at the name, and laughed even more at the story of Trifle and her feed bucket helmet.

Although Katy spent a lot of her time with Jacko, she was careful to give Trifle lots of attention too. She groomed the little pony regularly, and took her for walks around the farm on the lead rein so she'd get used to all the sights and sounds.

Every time Katy groomed Trifle, she inspected the pony's tail for white hairs and pulled a few suspect ones out. By the end of the summer, the top of Trifle's tail was looking rather bald.

"Is that pony getting sweet itch or something, Katy?" Granfer asked one day.

"What's sweet itch, Granfer?"

"An allergic reaction to midges. Ponies which suffer from it itch like crazy and often they develop bald patches. The latest thinking is that sweet itch can be inherited, so I wouldn't want to breed from a pony with it."

"Oh dear. Could a pony with sweet itch fail its inspection?"

"Well, I don't think it's actually an accepted reason for failing, but an inspector could advise against breeding, I suppose. It's a horrible disease with no known cure, although it can be managed in various ways. I'd be surprised if Trifle had it because, as far as I know, ponies from this herd don't suffer from sweet itch. But there's always a first time." Granfer examined Trifle. "Hmm, her mane seems fine. It looks a bit like over-enthusiastic tail-pulling to me. Exmoors shouldn't have their manes or tails pulled, Katy. You know that, don't you?" Granfer gave Katy a stern look which left her in no doubt that he knew what she had been up to.

"Sorry, Granfer. I'd forgotten," she said.

From that day on, Katy left Trifle's tail alone, although she inspected it anxiously for the appearance of white hairs. It was so difficult to tell what would be thought of as a white hair rather than a light-coloured one. All Exmoor pony manes and tails seemed to contain hairs of every shade of brown, from light sand to almost black. As branding day approached, the colour of Trifle's tail became the only thing Katy could think about.

Branding that year was on the Saturday before half term. Granfer was extremely worried. One of the inspectors had the reputation of being particularly strict, especially on the subject of white hairs. He was as nervous as Katy, but he was not going to use his position in the Exmoor Pony Society to plead a special case for the pony. Fate, and the inspectors, would decide.

Katy lay on her bed, hugging her pillow and praying. She couldn't bear to watch the inspection. If Trifle passed, she didn't want to see the branding, and if Trifle failed . . . Katy tried her best not to think about what would happen if Trifle failed. She repeated all the prayers that Gran had taught her and made up several herself, too. She also made some very rash promises like *I promise that I'll be good for ever if Trifle passes.*

Shall we start with the yearling filly that failed last year then, Jack?" asked Mr Wright, the secretary.

"Yes, good idea," Granfer replied. "At least she's halter broke, so she'll be a bit easier than the others," he added, trying to sound light-hearted. Were the inspectors aware of their tremendous power? With one simple decision they could change the destiny of a pony and the people who loved it.

"It was the tail that was the problem last year, wasn't it, Jack?" Alan, the inspector, asked.

"Yup, a few white baby hairs," Granfer replied. His voice sounded as if it belonged to someone else.

"Are you okay, Jack? Do you want me to get you a seat?" Mr Wright asked.

"No thanks, I'm fine."

"Well now, let's have a look at this tail, then," said Alan. "What d'you think, Mary?"

Mary was a hard, thin-faced woman with an extraordinary passion for Exmoor ponies. She'd been an inspector for years, and had very strong opinions about a lot of things, ponies included. "Someone's been doing a bit of tail-pulling, by the looks of it," she said, fixing her beady eyes on Granfer. "What's been going on here, Jack?"

Granfer felt like a schoolboy being accused of something he hadn't done. "That was my granddaughter who pulled her tail," he said quickly. "You know what these Pony Club children are like. She came back from camp with all these fancy ideas about pulling manes and tails, and didn't realise you should leave Exmoors natural. Luckily, I managed to stop her and explain before she tackled the mane."

To his surprise, Mary smiled. Perhaps she understood the situation. "Well, from the hairs I can see, she seems okay," she said. "What do you think, Alan?"

"Yes, okay by me," Alan replied. It would take a brave person to disagree with Mary.

"What numbers will we need for this one, then? A five for the herd mark on the shoulder, of course, but what about her own number?" Mary asked.

"Two-six-four was where we got to last year, so this one's two-six-five," said Granfer. He felt like hugging Mary, but thought he'd better not. He was being filmed by an Exmoor pony enthusiast with a video camera.

"Hasn't the Barton herd bred more than two hundred and sixty-five ponies?" asked the lady making the video.

"Oh yes. In fact, so many that, to avoid huge numbers, we had to start all over again at number one," Granfer explained.

Trifle was branded. She was now a registered Exmoor pony.

Two weeks later, Katy came back from school and went upstairs to change into her farm clothes. There was a white envelope on her bed with a printed address on it and something handwritten in blue ink to one side. She picked it up and pulled out the contents with trembling fingers. It was Trifle's Exmoor Pony Society passport. Barton Trifle was the name printed in the window on the front, and underneath was the registration number 5/265. Wonderfully grand and official. On the envelope Granfer had written:

Dear Katy. Keep this in a safe place - you'll need it when you go to shows. Much love, Granfer.

Katy looked at the passport for ages. Then she carefully put it under her pillow, and went to tell Trifle the good news.

"I know you don't understand about silly things like passports," she said, watching Trifle tuck into a celebratory feed of pony nuts and chopped apples. "Basically, it means that everything has turned out okay and you can stay here with Jacko and me forever. Oh, I do like happy endings!"

Trifle lifted her head out of the bucket and looked at Katy as if to say, "Well, you may think that this is where the story ends, but I know it's just the beginning."

Katy's Champion Pony, the second book in the trilogy, is available now.

Here is a preview of the first chapter.

1

Times Gone By

It was a typical winter's evening – chilly but not really cold, and drizzly but not really raining. Katy Squires and her best friend, Alice, stood in the old cow shed which had been converted into stables for Katy's two ponies at her home, Barton Farm. The girls leaned on the wall inside the shed and chatted as they watched the ponies eat their hay.

Jacko was a liver chestnut gelding. He was fourteen hands high, ten years old and lovely to ride. Somehow he was cheeky and fun but at the same time kind and dependable. Katy had loved him from the first time she'd ridden him at Stonyford Riding Stables. Her Granfer had bought him for her as a surprise birthday present.

Trifle was a registered Exmoor filly who'd been born on the moor above Barton Farm on Katy's birthday nearly three years ago. Katy had secretly bought her from Brendon pony sale. It was hard to imagine that the sturdy, confident pony munching away without a care in the world had, not so long ago, been a timid wild foal. Katy had brought Trifle back to where she belonged, and the little pony seemed to know it.

Jacko and Trifle had been at Barton for nearly two years now, and Katy couldn't imagine life without them. She looked at the contented ponies, breathed in the wonderful stable smell and felt pure happiness envelop her like a warm blanket.

"Look how fluffy Trifle's winter coat is," Katy said. "She looks like a life-sized cuddly toy, doesn't she?"

Trifle seemed to realise she'd become the centre of attention. She stopped eating, came to Katy and nuzzled her jacket affectionately.

Alice laughed. "Do you remember Mum winning that huge teddy in the raffle at the New Year's Eve party last year? Be careful, Trifle, or Katy will give you away as a raffle prize tonight."

Katy put her hands over Trifle's furry ears. "Don't listen to silly old Auntie Alice," she said. "For starters, you'd never get up all those steps in the Town Hall, would you?"

"Oh well, Trifle," Alice said. "You'll just have to stay here and have a stable sleepover with Jacko." She turned to Katy. "Have you made any New Year's resolutions yet?"

"Mmm. I suppose I ought to," Katy replied. "I wish I didn't like chocolate so much and I want to win lots of rosettes. Oh yes, and I'd love Trifle to become a champion Exmoor pony, of course."

"Are those wishes or resolutions? A resolution is something you're going to do, not something you wish would happen."

Katy gave her friend a light punch on the arm. "Oh, you're such a know-it-all, Alice Gardner! They're a bit of both, I suppose. So what are your resolutions, clever-clogs?"

"Okay. My resolution is to try to be nice to my terrible twin brothers, and my wish is that I'll be happy when we move to new schools next year after the summer holidays."

"I shouldn't worry about that, Alice. We'll all be going together, so at least we'll know some people already. You always seem to get on with everybody, anyway, so you'll be all right."

"Um . . . there's something I've been meaning to tell you, Katy."

Katy was unconcerned. "Well, tell me quickly because we'd better go and get ready for the party."

"I'm going to a different school. A boarding school miles away."

"Oh, Alice! How awful for you!"

"No, you don't understand. I *want* to go."

"But I thought we were best friends," Katy mumbled.

"Of course we are, and we can stay best friends too. We'll still see each other in the holidays, and we can text each other and things, can't we?"

"No we can't! I haven't got a mobile phone, have I? There's no signal here at the farm, remember?" Katy said, angry now. Alice *knew* she didn't have a mobile phone! She also knew it was the one thing Katy really wanted. Not having one made her feel left out at school, but her parents said it would be a waste of money.

"Sorry, I forgot. Okay, we can email each other. Chat on Facebook. I mean, there's lots of ways of keeping in touch."

"It won't be the same, though, will it? Can't you just say you've changed your mind and you don't want to go?"

"Are you crazy? Think what my parents would say!" Alice exclaimed. "Besides, I really do want to go there. I've been for an interview and everything, and it's *such* a cool place. They do loads of games, and they've got amazing stables, with an indoor school and a cross-country course. And there's a big forest nearby with lots of sandy tracks for riding. You can even take your own pony and keep it at livery. It costs extra, but Dad says he doesn't mind paying for me to take Shannon. Isn't that great? His new house is quite near the school, too, and I'll be able to go there for weekends. I've hardly seen him since he split up with Mum, and I do miss him a lot. So I'm really excited about it, actually. I wish you could come too though. You with Jacko and me with Shannon – just think what fun we'd have!"

Alice's tactless enthusiasm cut into Katy. Before she could stop herself she blurted out, "Well, thanks for rubbing it in."

Alice looked bewildered. "Rubbing what in?"

"You *know* that my mum and dad would never be able to afford a boarding school. They're not rich like your family!" Tears started to run down Katy's cheeks. She turned and ran out of the shed.

"Katy! Come back. I didn't mean it like that." Alice called after her.

"I don't want to talk about it!" Katy shouted into the damp night. She was vaguely aware she was being unfair but she was too upset to care, and it was much easier to get angry about things like mobile phones and money than talk about her true feelings. For the past year or so she and Alice had been inseparable friends, both at school and in the holidays. The thought of being parted for weeks – months even – was dreadful, but Alice obviously didn't feel the same way. Why couldn't she see how much that hurt?

The New Year's Eve party was in the local Town Hall. There was a barn dance for all ages, with a band and a caller who told everybody what they should be doing. Some people knew the steps already and others got in terrible muddles, but it didn't matter. The main idea was that everyone got together and had a good time.

To begin with Katy tried to avoid Alice, but it became impossible – especially when Mum and Dad went off to sit at a table with Alice's mum, Melanie.

It was Alice who broke the ice. She came up and said, "I'm sorry, Katy. I didn't mean to. I mean I don't want you to think . . . oh – you know what I mean!"

Katy still felt betrayed. She wanted to say, *Yes, I know what you mean: you'd rather go miles away to a posh boarding school than stay here and go to the local school with me. I thought we were best friends, but you've ruined everything!* Instead, she said, "Yeah, well, it's okay. Let's just forget about it, shall we?"

Alice gave her a quick hug. "I knew you'd understand!" she said. "Friends for ever?"

"Friends for ever," Katy replied, trying her best to smile.

Alice grabbed her hand and headed towards their parents, who were beckoning to them. "Come on!" She said. "They need us to make up numbers for the next dance."

It was hard to be unhappy with all the music, dancing and laughter.

Next autumn is ages away, Katy thought. Too far away to worry about now.

They stayed on the dance floor for several more dances until the caller announced, "Take your partners for The West Country Waltz!"

"Let's sit this one out. It sounds complicated, and I'm done in," Katy said to Alice.

They went back to the table where Katy's Gran and Granfer were sitting.

Alice collapsed onto a chair in a mock faint. "We're shattered!" she announced.

"Pah!" Granfer scoffed. "Young people don't have any stamina nowadays. Come on Peggy, love. We'd better show them how it's done." He took Gran's hand and led her onto the dance floor.

"How embarrassing!" Katy whispered to Alice, but her embarrassment soon turned into amazement.

Gran and Granfer danced gracefully and in perfect harmony, their feet hardly touching the floor. People stood and watched in awe as the couple swept round the room with breathtaking style.

"I had no idea Granfer could dance like that, and how does Gran manage with her arthritis?" Katy asked her father.

"When Gran gets her dancing shoes on, nothing stops her," Dad answered. "Gran and Granfer used to win all sorts of prizes for their dancing when they were younger. The money they won helped them to turn Barton into one of the best farms on Exmoor."

For the first time, Katy imagined her grandparents as a handsome young couple with their whole lives in front of them, long before they were Gran and Granfer, or even Mum and Dad.

The music stopped, and everybody burst into applause.

Soon it was midnight, and everyone was hugging and kissing and saying, "Happy New Year!" Then they formed a huge circle, held hands with crossed arms and sang *Auld Lang Syne*.

Katy was sandwiched between Alice and Granfer, diving in and out of the circle in a long, snake-like chain as they sang the chorus.

"What on earth does Auld Lang Syne mean?" Katy asked Granfer afterwards.

"Roughly translated, it means times gone by, I think," Granfer explained. "It's Scottish, but over the years it seems to have become a traditional New Year's Eve song all over the place, probably because it tells about how time goes on but friendships should be remembered." He paused, and sighed deeply. "Yes, whatever happens, friends and family should never be forgotten."

A forlorn expression came over him, and for a dreadful moment Katy thought he might cry. Perhaps he'd overheard her row with Alice. She accidentally caught Alice's eye, and looked away quickly.

Luckily, Melanie appeared with a tray of drinks. "The glasses with stems are champagne and the tumblers are lemonade," she said.

Granfer handed Katy and Alice tumblers, and took a couple of glasses of champagne for Gran and himself. "Thanks, Melanie," he said. He raised his glass and smiled. "To times gone by!"

"To times gone by!" the girls repeated. Katy took a sip of lemonade, and the bubbles went up her nose.

The Squires family got home from the party in the early hours of the morning. Gran and Granfer stayed at Barton Farm for the night so they didn't have to drive back to their bungalow.

Mum had just finished cooking breakfast the following morning when the telephone rang.

Dad sat at the kitchen table, eating his eggs and bacon. "Who on earth could be ringing at this time of day?" he grumbled. "My New Year's resolution is to ignore the phone at meal times."

Mum gestured to him to be quiet. "Barton Farm. Can I help you? Oh! Hello, Rachel. Happy New Year to you too. What? Well, that's marvellous news! Congratulations! I'm thrilled for you both. Jack and Peggy are here, so do you want a quick word? We'll see you soon. Okay. Love and congratulations to Mark. Bye, now." She handed the phone to Granfer.

"Hello, Rachel love. Well done. I expect you want to speak to Mum, then. Yes, you too. Take care, now," Granfer said.

Gran took the handset from Granfer. "Hello? Congratulations, darling! I'm so pleased. What? Yes, of course Dad's pleased too. He's just, you know, it takes a bit of time . . . Yes, I know. Oh, how lovely . . ."

"What's going on?" Katy whispered.

"Auntie Rachel and Mark are engaged," Mum whispered back.

"Wow! They're getting married?" Katy exclaimed.

"Ssshhhh!" Mum and Dad hissed together.

"There's too much noise in here, Rachel. I'll just go into the hall," Gran said, giving the family one of her stern looks.

With Gran talking in the hall, everyone talked more

normally in the kitchen, although they were secretly trying to eavesdrop on Gran's conversation at the same time.

"You were a bit short on the phone, Jack," Mum said to Granfer.

"Oh, you know me. I hate talking on that contraption," Granfer said. "I'm very happy for them both. Delighted. Over the moon."

Katy sensed Granfer wasn't nearly as happy as he made out. She knew how fond he was of his only daughter, and guessed it was hard for him to let go, even though Mark and Rachel had been going out for ages and everyone had assumed they'd get married one day. The idea took some getting used to, she had to admit. For a start, it was bound to mean Rachel would spend less time at Barton Farm. Since Katy had become the proud owner of Trifle and Jacko she'd grown to rely on her aunt's visits. Looking after two ponies was an awesome responsibility, and Rachel seemed to have all the answers to Katy's frequent questions.

"You're what? You can't be! When? That soon? Oh dear! Yes, of course it's a great opportunity, but..." Gran's voice became alarmed.

In the kitchen they all fell silent, straining to hear what she was saying.

A few minutes later she returned to the kitchen,

looking flustered. "Oh dear! I can't believe it!"

Dad leaped up and helped her to her chair. "Can't believe what?" he asked. "That Rachel's getting married at long last?"

"No, of course not! We all expected that! No… Oh dear, I don't know how to tell you this, so I'll just have to come out with it straight. Rachel says Mark's uncle has offered him a job running a huge cattle station in Australia. They're going to live out there just as soon as they're married. They're moving to Australia this summer! Oh dear!"

Granfer got up from his chair and put his arm round Gran's slumped shoulders. "Don't take it so hard, love. It'll be okay. We'll go out and see them, if you like. It's not far nowadays. I've always fancied a trip down under."

Gran looked up at him with watery eyes. "You knew, didn't you? How come you knew?"

Granfer forced a smile, but his face looked sad. "Mark came to see me yesterday to ask for our daughter's hand in marriage. Very proper and correct, as always. He told me then. Said I wasn't to breathe a word to anyone until he'd asked Rachel to marry him."

Now Katy understood why Granfer had looked so sad last night when he'd said friends and family should never be forgotten.

*

I don't like this year much, Katy thought as she put the ponies out in the field later that morning. What other surprises has it got in store?

She watched as Jacko and Trifle cantered off together.

Alice had promised to be her best friend forever, and Rachel had promised to help her train Trifle, but they'd either forgotten or didn't care. Both had made different plans for the future, and Katy had no part in them. She remembered raising a glass to times gone by a few hours ago. Time moves on and people move on with it, she thought sadly. What if friendships aren't remembered? What if Alice and Auntie Rachel make new lives for themselves and forget about me? How on earth am I going to cope without them?

Author's Note

Many ideas for my books about Katy and Trifle have come from real life. For instance, I live with my family on an Exmoor hill farm and we have a herd of free-living Exmoor ponies, so although Barton Farm is fictional it has many things in common with my home. Stonyford is also fictional, but the villages in this story do exist – so does Exmoor, which is a very beautiful National Park in the south west of England. Oh, and I go to Brendon pony sale most years, but so far I haven't secretly bought a pony . . .

All the human and equine characters in this book are

fictional, but they're a combination of my imagination and some of the people and ponies I've known throughout my life. They take shape in my head and then seem to develop a life of their own. That's when writing becomes really exciting!

Of the ponies which have helped me with this book, a Welsh cob called Jacko and two Exmoor ponies called Nipper and Tinkerbell deserve a special mention.

I saw Nipper just after he'd been born on the moor above our farm. It was a bitterly cold afternoon in April, and I was so worried about him that I visited him regularly. He seemed to trust me from the start and he used to come running up for a cuddle, despite the fact his mother didn't trust people at all. Our children called him Nipper because if you gave his back a rub he'd try to return the favour, like ponies do when they groom each other, but unfortunately he had rather sharp teeth! My experiences with Nipper gave me the initial ideas for this story.

Jacko was my first pony, and he was just as wonderful as the Jacko in this book. He was a handsome liver chestnut Welsh cob, and he was the pony I loved most in the world when I was a girl.

Tinkerbell, who still lives here at the farm, was our daughter Sarah's pony when they were both much younger. She taught Sarah the importance of bravery and a non-slip saddle pad, amongst other things, and both she and Sarah gave me lots of ideas for these stories about Katy and Trifle. Our herd of free-living Exmoor ponies, which we keep on the moorland above our farm, have also provided me with a great deal of inspiration.

Over the years I've handled several of our Exmoor ponies as weaned foals, wild off the moor. I've learned a great deal from the ponies themselves, and also from a natural horsewoman called Vanessa Bee. All the mistakes Katy makes, when she's handling Trifle in this story, I've made myself – except our pony got a bucket of water, not pony nuts, stuck on her head! I used Katy's "Rome wasn't built in a day" method of taming wild foals for several years until I discovered natural horsemanship, which makes communication with horses a lot easier.

It's hard to mention individual people for fear of leaving someone out, but friends who have given me particular help and encouragement are Marcia Monbleau, Sally Chapman-Walker, Sue Baker and Sue Croft and, of course, my mum.

Most of all, thanks and love to Chris, my very patient and understanding husband, and our children, George and Sarah. Chris has supported me in countless ways, including providing illustrations for this book.

Last, but not least, many thanks to Fiona Kennedy, Felicity Johnston and the team at Orion for all their invaluable guidance and hard work.

Victoria Eveleigh
North Devon
September 2011

Exmoor Ponies

Exmoor ponies, or "Exmoors" as they are often called, are a very special breed. They are the only native pony breed that has the same characteristics as the original British Hill Pony that came to the British Isles about one hundred and thirty thousand years ago. Various studies of the bones, teeth and genetics of Exmoor ponies have supported this.

Why Exmoor ponies have survived as nature intended, whereas other breeds have been altered by man, is a bit of a mystery. Historically, Exmoor was a wild, sparsely populated area, which was reserved as a Royal Forest or hunting ground. There were no significant trade routes through the area, and no important towns nearby. It seems that, because of this, Exmoor had little contact with the rest of Britain and the wild ponies within the Forest remained an isolated, pure population.

In 1818, the Forest was sold to an industrialist

called John Knight. Several local farmers bought some of the wild ponies and started up herds of their own, including the former warden of Exmoor Forest, Sir Thomas Acland. He founded the Acland herd, now the Anchor herd, which can be seen on Winsford Hill.

The Exmoor Pony Society was founded in 1921, with the purpose of keeping the breed true to type.

During the Second World War, many ponies were stolen for food and fewer ponies were bred. In the end, only about forty-six mares and four stallions were left on Exmoor. A remarkable lady called Mary Etherington encouraged some Exmoor farmers to re-establish their herds so that the breed was saved. However, it is still classified as endangered by the Rare Breeds Survival Trust.

Exmoor ponies make history come to life. It is up to all of us to ensure they have a future.

If you'd like to find out more about Exmoor ponies, the Exmoor Pony Society has a very good website www.exmoorponysociety.org.uk with lots of information and details of ponies for sale or loan. The secretary is called Sue McGeever, and her telephone number is (01884) 839930.

A visit to Exmoor isn't complete without a trip to the Exmoor Pony Centre, near Dulverton. This is the headquarters of the Moorland Mousie Trust, a charity dedicated to the welfare and promotion of Exmoor ponies. Admission to see the ponies and their pony-themed gift shop is free, but you can also book pony handling sessions for beginners or rides on the moor for experienced riders. For details see the website www.exmoorponycentre.org.uk or telephone (01398) 323093. The Trust runs a pony adoption scheme – the next best thing to owning an Exmoor pony!

the
orion star

CALLING ALL GROWN-UPS!
Sign up for **the orion star** newsletter to
hear about your favourite authors and exclusive
competitions, plus details of how children
can join our 'Story Stars' review panel.

Sign up at:
www.orionbooks.co.uk/orionstar

Follow us  @the_orionstar
Find us ☐ facebook.com/TheOrionStar